SHATTERED WORLD III
CHINA

SHATTERED WORLD III
CHINA

Scott M. Baker

Also by Scott M. Baker

Novels
Nurse Alissa vs. the Zombies
Nurse Alissa vs. the Zombies II: Escape
Shattered World I: Paris
Shattered World II: Russia
The Vampire Hunters
Vampyrnomicon
Dominion
Rotter World
Rotter Nation
Rotter Apocalypse
Yeitso

Novellas
Nazi Ghouls From Space
Twilight of the Living Dead
This Is Why We Can't Have Nice Things During the Zombie Apocalypse

Anthologies
Cruise of the Living Dead and other Stories
Incident on Ironstone Lane and Other Horror Stories

A Schattenseite Book

Shattered World III: China
by Scott M. Baker.
Copyright © 2020. All Rights Reserved.
Print Edition

ISBN-13: 978-0-9963121-8-9

Cover Art © by Joolz & Jarling – Uwe Jarling & Julie Nicholls 2020
Editing © Michele Thompson 2018
Map © Petar Dekic 2020

To my father

He was a simple man of simple means who had one goal in life – to make sure his children were happy and successful. He did a great job on both counts. We love you and miss you.

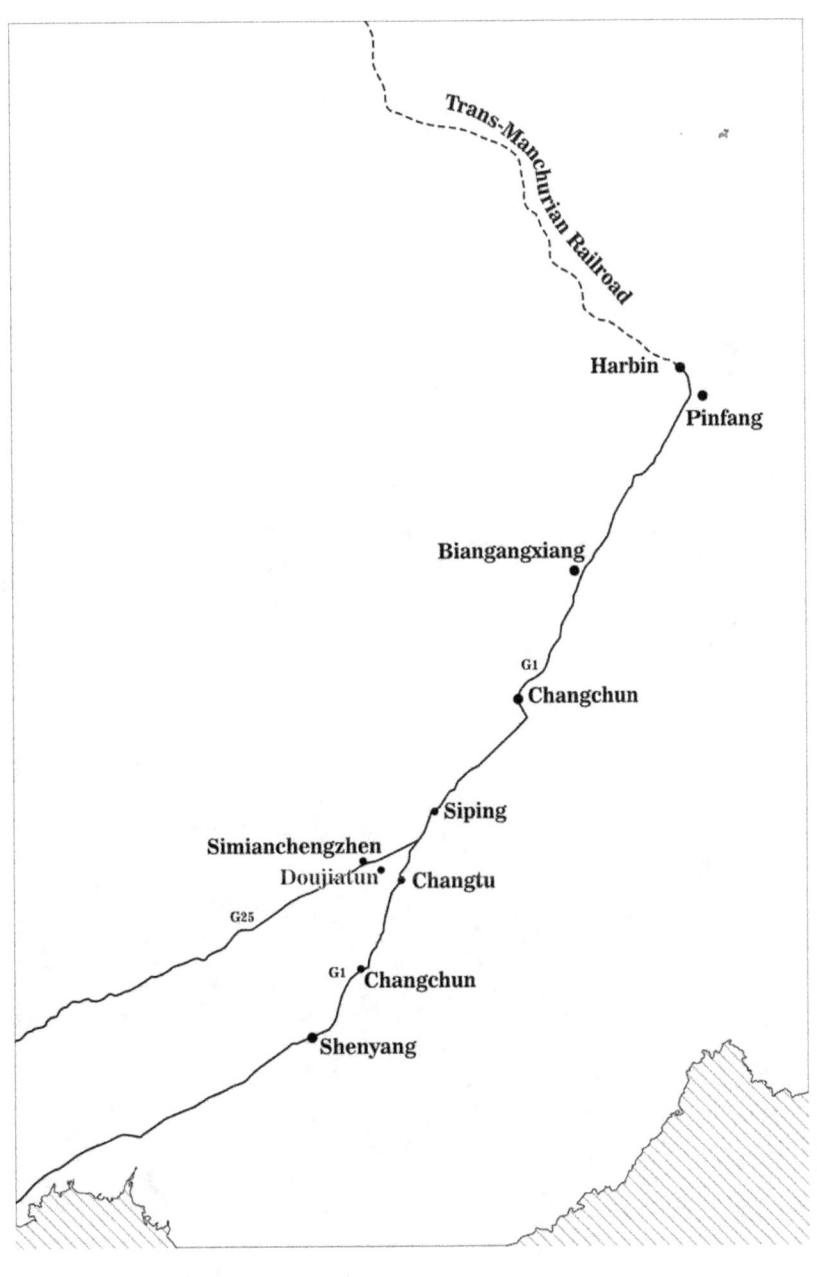

BOOK ONE

CHAPTER ONE

A small village, twenty-five miles north of Chang-chun, Jilin Province, China
The day after the closure of the portal in Siberia

LITTLE AH REMEMBERED the times before the end of humanity. Being only five years old she did not recall much, only the important things like watching television, playing with her toys, meeting her friends in pre-school, sleeping in a warm bed, and always having enough to eat. It had been over a year since the electricity went out and ten months since her parents had abandoned their apartment in Changchun and headed into the country in search of food. By now, Ah had grown accustomed to sleeping on the ground under a worn and dirty blanket, living inside of a tent that only partially kept out the rain and the cold, and eating whatever scraps the villagers could scrounge up that day. She did not enjoy her new life; she had only become used to it. She missed her favorite cartoons, her soft mattress, and hot meals at the table with her family. Most of all, she missed those times when her parents were happy. Although Ah's mother remained cheerful during the day, she cried at night when she thought her daughter had fallen asleep. Her father was the same way, always smiling and rubbing her hair, telling her things might be bad now but would soon improve. Ah grinned and nodded to make her father feel good but deep down she knew things would not get better. She could see the fear and worry in his eyes and decided to make the best of the situation and not upset her parents. Her old life was gone and would never return.

Ah pulled the smelly blanket under her chin and rested her head on the backpack she used as a pillow. She had kept only one connection to those happier, earlier times—Ling Ling, a stuffed panda, the only possession her parents allowed her to bring when they left home. Ling Ling had seen better days. One of her eyes had fallen out and the white fur had become so dirty it blended with the black. For Ah, the stuffed panda was priceless because it comforted her through the uncertainty. She confided in it when she did not want to bother her mother or father. She cried on it when she was sad, or clutched it tight when afraid, both of which happened much more frequently than she cared to admit. Ah kissed the top of Ling Ling's head before going to sleep. She would rather die than leave her panda behind.

A loud commotion outside the tent woke her up. She sat upright, clutching the stuffed animal to her chest. Yelling came from around the camp site and people raced back and forth. In the distance, she heard galloping horses, the noise becoming more intense with each passing second. Someone barked an order about defending the perimeter. Gun fire erupted. It lasted for several minutes and mixed with screams. Then, as suddenly as the uproar began, everything went quiet except for the sound of running footsteps approaching the tent. Ah tried to remain brave, but her body shivered from fear.

The flap flew aside as Ah's mother raced in and rushed over to her daughter. "We have to get going."

"Where?"

"Don't ask questions." Her mother's voice wavered. She grabbed Ah by her left wrist and yanked her toward the exit. Ah dropped Ling Ling. Breaking free from her mother, the child ran back and picked up the stuffed panda.

"Hurry up," her mother snapped.

Ah hugged Ling Ling and joined her mother. Before they could exit, a man carrying a large gun used the barrel to push aside the flap and enter. He wore a uniform that Ah recognized as belonging to the People's Liberation Army, or PLA. Her mother gasped and stepped backward, dragging Ah with her. She wrapped her arms around her daughter and cried. "Please don't hurt us."

The soldier stared at them, his face expressionless. Turning his head, he waved for someone to join them. Ah's mother gripped her tightly and sobbed.

A young woman entered the tent. She wore civilian clothes—leather pants, a white shirt, and a tan leather jacket, none of which were soiled or tattered. Her raven black hair hung past her shoulders, clean and well groomed. She stood five and a half feet in height and, although by no means overweight, she did not have that emaciated appearance the others in camp did. Her deep brown eyes switched between Ah and her mother. After a few seconds, the woman smiled. "My name is Mei. Please, don't be afraid. We're here to help you."

"You shot at us," growled Ah's mother.

"Your people shot first." Mei's pleasant demeanor did not falter. "We only defended ourselves. Now please, gather your belongings and follow me."

"Suppose we want to stay here?"

"I'm sorry. We can't allow anyone to stay behind."

When Ah's mother refused to budge, Mei moved across the tent and squatted in front of the child. "What's your name?"

"Ah." She hugged the stuffed panda.

"That's a beautiful name." Mei reached toward Ah. Her mother held her close but Mei showed no interest in the child. She petted the panda's head. "What's her name?"

"Ling Ling."

"Do you trust me, Ah? Do you think I intend to hurt you or your mother?"

For some reason, Ah did not feel threatened by this woman. Maybe it was Mei's joyful expression, or maybe the glint in her eyes that promised her intentions were in everyone's best interest. Ah swallowed hard. "I trust you."

"Good." Mei grinned. "Do you and Ling Ling want to come with me?"

Ah glanced up at her mother. "Can we go with her?"

Her mother trembled and, for a moment, Ah thought she might cry. Finally, she gave in to the inevitable. "Promise me you won't harm Ah."

"I promise," Mei said with sincerity.

Taking Ah by the right hand, her mother headed for the exit. Mei and the PLA soldier moved aside, each holding up one end of the flap. Once outside, they followed Mei to a clearing on the western perimeter. Most of the people from the camp were present, while a group of people she did not know, each carrying a gun, stood behind and on either side of them. Ah searched for her father but could not find him. She wondered if he was one of the bodies lying scattered around the field. Before she could ask her mother, something in front of them caught her attention.

Three horses approached camp, one in front and two slightly behind and on either side. The figures riding the rearmost horses wore black cowls that covered their hands and extended below the stirrups. They bowed forward in their saddles so that the hoods draped over their faces and hands. The rider of the lead horse wore a similar cowl, only blood red. Thirty feet from the group, the last two horses stopped. The animals shook their heads and stamped their hooves; the drivers remained motionless, as if there they were not alive. The first horse continued ahead and stopped directly in front of Ah. As the rider dismounted and approached, Ah tried to get a look under the cowl but the features remained hidden in the shadows. Mei spoke loud enough for everyone to hear.

"Ladies and gentlemen, this is Bai, the head of our group. She will lead you to the Promised Land. All you have to do is trust her, like we do."

A flurry of questions followed Mei's statement as those in the group asked at once where they were going, how long it would take, and what they could expect when they arrived. Mei calmed them down when Ah asked, "Are you going to hurt us?"

"We're going to save you."

"Save us from what?" asked Ah's mother.

"From all of this." Mei gestured toward the camp site. "We're going to save you from discomfort and starvation, and from the *Xiongnu*. The world as you once knew it has come to an end. Things will never return to what they used to be. We're creating a new way of life and are giving you the opportunity to join us and make this world a better place. You can stay here if you want, cuddling in fear and living like vermin. Or you can come with us and have a purpose."

Ah stepped forward. "Is Ling Ling invited to join?"

Mei began to speak but Bai raised her right hand, cutting her off. Ah caught a glimpse of Bai's fingers and shuddered. She wanted to run away. Then Bai spoke, her voice soft and reassuring, mesmerizing yet unsettling at the same time. "Who is Ling Ling, my child?"

Ah held up he stuffed panda.

Bai reached out and rubbed her forefinger along Ah's cheek. This time the child did not flinch. "Everyone is welcome into this new realm."

Ah grinned and hugged her panda.

Bai remounted her horse, turned it around, and headed back the way she had come. As she passed, the other two horses fell in line behind her. Mei motioned for the others to follow. Ah surged forward, dragging along her mother. One by one, the others followed until the entire camp was on the march toward their new destiny.

CHAPTER TWO

The Trans-Siberian Railroad, ten miles west of Harbin, Heilongjiang Province, China
One day later

JASON MCCREARY SHIFTED on the pile of hay to get into a more comfortable position. Lucifer did not notice the movement, despite his stomach being used as a pillow. The werehound continued snoring. Lilith, who had been cuddling beside Jason, whimpered as her master rolled over. When he settled down, she inched her way over until she sidled up against his back. A few minutes passed before Lilith's breathing grew shallow. Jason envied his pets. He wished he could sleep as soundly as they did.

Closing his eyes, he allowed the rhythmic clacking of the wheels and gentle sway of the stock car to lull him. Resting had been difficult enough with everyone on the train crammed into the sole surviving sleeper, so he had opted to camp out in the rolling stock that transported the team's horses. However, even the relative quiet of this space had not helped. He was not bothered by the overpowering smell of dung and the constant neighing and snorting of the horses. In fact, he found it soothing. Jason could not rest because his mind raced.

After closing the interdimensional portal in Paris three months ago, Jason had formed a new team, comprised mostly of survivors of the first mission, to travel around the world and close the remaining four. Their first destination had been Moscow. Meeting up with the Russians in Minsk had been fortuitous because it gave his team the resources and manpower necessary to defeat the demons guarding the portal in Red Square and shut it down. Unfortunately, their victory celebration had been short-lived. In the first few days of the apocalypse, the Russians had attempted to close the portal with a nuclear device, failing in the misguided effort and inadvertently punching open a second one near the Siberian town of Irkutsk along the shores of Lake Baikal. General Zhirinovsky, the leader of the enclave, had offered the services of his own private, heavily-armed train to protect Jason's team on their journey east. Even this mode of transportation had proved sorely lacking against what they faced in Siberia. A hundred ravagers guarded the portal. Every time Jason closed his eyes, he recalled images from the battle. How the demons had swarmed the train, tearing through it and ripping apart anyone who got in their way. How they had derailed most of the sleeper cars, forcing his team and the Russians to fight the Demon Spawn in brutal hand-to-hand combat. How Sasha had mounted the anti-matter device on the lead steam engine and rode it into the gate, using her minigun to clear the Golem blocking the tracks.

Jason lost several good people in Russia, and their faces haunted his dreams. Reinhard, who had been with the team from their first raid into Paris, had sacrificed himself in Red Square to save the others, being engulfed by dragon fire. Werner, who had once been a member of the protective force defending Mont St. Michel before joining Jason's team, had been torn apart by ravagers while helping others escape from the overturned sleeper cars. Neal, who should never have gone with them in the first place, but who was the only medic they could find following Doc's death in Paris, had died protecting the anti-matter devices. And, of course, Sasha, although technically she did not die near Irkutsk because she previously had been killed in Paris and resurrected from Purgatory to come back to Earth and help close the portals. Jason knew he would be reunited again with Sasha.

It was the only certainty he could rely on.

His team had extinguished three portals and traveled across Eurasia, an impressive accomplishment, yet Jason could not rest on his laurels. Doc had created six anti-matter devices to close the five known portals, and three of them already had been used. Discovering the existence of the second portal in Russia had been an unwelcome surprise because that required him to use his only spare. If any more portals existed that he did not know about, or if one of the remaining devices malfunctioned, their mission would have been for nothing. Even if one remained open, it could spew out enough Demon Spawn to eventually overrun the planet. If those concerns did not generate enough stress, Jason still had no indication of the exact location of the remaining portals, just vague references that they existed in northeast China, Japan, and somewhere along the east coast of the United States. Nor did he have any idea of how he would get to Japan and, more importantly, how he would cross the Pacific Ocean to reach the United States. When all these variables were factored together, Jason wondered how he got any sleep.

Physical exhaustion eventually won out and Jason dozed off. He awoke when the train lurched to a halt. Lucifer and Lilith raised their heads, their ears perked up for signs of danger. Jason sat up in the hay, his heart racing and his insides tightening as his body went into fight-or-flight mode. He listened, expecting to hear gunfire, the cries of men coming under attack, or the screeching of demons. Thankfully, the only sounds were the rustling of the horses as they moved about their stalls. A few minutes later, the door at the far end of the stock car slid open, and someone approached, not running or panicked, but walking casually. Jeanette appeared in the opening of the stall and leaned against the jamb. Her face beamed.

"Well, you're finally awake."

"What do you mean?" Jason ran a hand through his hair.

"I've barely slept since we left Lake Baikal."

Jeanette chuckled. "I have news for you. You've been asleep for almost eighteen hours."

"You're kidding."

"I'm afraid not. You missed dinner *and* breakfast."

"I don't feel rested."

"That's because you're exhausted. You'll feel better once you've been up awhile."

Jason lifted his arms behind his head and stretched them on either side. "How do you know how long I've been asleep?"

"I checked on you every few hours. Each time I came by you were dead to the world and didn't even acknowledge me."

"Wow." At least that explained why his dreams were so vivid. "You could have joined me."

Jeanette shook her head. "I love you, Jason, though not enough to sleep in the hay when there's a perfectly comfortable bed a few cars down. Besides, there was no room."

Lucifer barked once. Lilith leaned her head back and gave Jason three licks on the face. He scratched each of them behind the ears and got to his feet. "Why did we stop?"

"I don't know. Svetlana sent me to get you. She wants us at the front of the train."

Jason let Jeanette lead the way. Lucifer and Lilith fell in behind them. Colonel Svetlana Yakolevna Krayevsky stood by the cowcatcher of the LV class steam locomotive. A wind blowing from the south folded her chest-length red hair across her face, partially hiding the scar that ran down her features and the black patch covering her left eye. Svetlana focused her attention on the tracks ahead of her.

As Jason approached, he asked, "Have we reached Harbin?"

"We've reached the end of the line, my friend."

He followed her gaze. A one-hundred-foot segment of track had been systematically destroyed. The rails had been removed and the wooden ties dug up, placed in a pile, and set on fire.

The rails had then been thrown on top of the flames. Two had bent from the heat, rendering them useless.

"There's no way to repair this," said Svetlana. "Thankfully, we're less than ten miles from Harbin, so you'll be able to continue on foot."

Jason studied the damaged segment of rail line. "They did a thorough job."

"Obviously someone in Harbin doesn't want visitors," said Jeanette.

Svetlana shook her head. "I'm more concerned that someone in Harbin doesn't want its citizens getting out."

TEN MINUTES LATER, Jason and Jeanette stood in the command car around the remnants of a rectangular table that served as the conference table. Joining them were Haneef, Jason's second in command; Father Belsario, the head of the Purgatoriati, who examined the others with his cold brown eyes; and Dr. Ustagov, the Russian scientist who accompanied them as a medic. Svetlana rummaged through her white metal desk, eventually pulling a map from the drawer. As the colonel crossed over to the others, she folded the edges underneath to expose the central portion and placed it on the corner of the table that had not been damaged. Jason frowned. All the places names were printed in Chinese characters and Cyrillic.

Svetlana pointed to the large city near the top edge of the map. "This is Harbin. We're ten miles southwest of the city's train station." She ran her finger along the main road leading south from the city. Two major population centers sat along that route. As her finger passed each point, she said, "This is Changchun. This is Shenyang. According to our best information, the portal is somewhere between Harbin and Shenyang, and is within a twenty-mile radius of this corridor."

"Where does that information come from?" Jason asked.

"When we left for Siberia, General Zhirinovsky began asking around on the radio to find out if anyone knew anything that could help on this leg of your expedition. A PLA contingent held up in an underground bunker outside of Beijing radioed us back. The Chinese sent out several recon patrols to determine its exact location, and none of them have been heard from. They did, however, agree to give it one more try."

"When will they get back to us?" asked Father Belsario.

Svetlana shook her head. "They won't. More accurately, if they do, we won't know about it."

"I don't understand," said Jeanette.

Svetlana motioned for Ustagov to answer. The doctor removed his reading glasses and tapped one arm against his lower lip. "The closer we get to Harbin, the more sporadic our radio signals have been. We lost all contact with Moscow early this morning. I assume it has something to do with the fact that the closer we get to the Chinese portal the greater is the interference."

"It doesn't matter," said Jason. He pointed to the Harbin-Changchun-Shenyang road on the map. "If it's anywhere along this route, we'll find it."

"It shouldn't take you long," said Svetlana. "By horse, it will take you two to three weeks to reach Shenyang."

"Good. The sooner we can get this over with the better."

Svetlana folded the map and handed it to Jason. "You'll need this more than I do."

"Thanks, but I can't read Russian or Chinese."

"You don't have to. The doctor can translate for you."

"One of the many services I provide," said Ustagov, attempting to be humorous.

Svetlana cast the doctor a disapproving glare before continuing. "Even though you have only a two- to three-week trip ahead of you, I'm giving your team most of our supplies."

"What will you do for food?" asked Father Belsario.

"There's only four of us left so we can go on reduced rations for the trip home. You have no idea what you'll find in China, so you can use it more than we can. I'm also trading weapons with your people."

"Why do that? Our weapons work fine."

"Your weapons are FAMAS automatic rifles, which use 5.56mm NATO rounds. You'll be hard pressed to find replacement ammunition in China. The 7.62mm rounds for our AK-47s are common throughout this part of Asia, so it'll be easier for you to restock."

"Won't you need them?" asked Jeanette.

The colonel shook her head. "Thanks to you, I doubt we'll run into any difficulties on the way back."

"I appreciate it."

Svetlana nodded. "I'm also giving you our winter coats."

"I can't ask you to do that."

"You're not asking. I'm volunteering." When Jason opened his mouth to protest, Svetlana raised her hand and cut him off. "I don't want any arguments. It's already getting cold in Manchuria. In a couple of weeks, it'll be winter, and without heavy clothing, you won't survive long."

Jason relented because he knew everything Svetlana said made sense. In a week, the colonel and her men would be back in Moscow: God only knew how long Jason's team would be on the move. "I don't know how to thank you."

"You already have by closing down the portals in Moscow and Irkutsk. All of Russia is grateful. This is the least we can do."

Jason blushed. Jeanette reached out and squeezed his hand.

Svetlana checked her watch. "It'll be dark in six hours. Do you want to spend the night here and head out in the morning?"

"No. I don't want to waste any time. If we move now, we can make it to the outskirts of Harbin by nightfall and set up camp there, and then clear the city while we have a full day of sunlight tomorrow."

"I can't argue with that." Svetlana banged her right hand on the table. "I'll have my men get your horses ready."

JASON LEANED AGAINST the armored steam engine's cowcatcher, overseeing the preparations for departure. Except for the Purgatoriati, who wore their breastplates and cloaks, and Dr. Ustagov, who sported a Spetsnaz four-color camouflage uniform, each of his team was dressed in the same green flightsuits they had started out with from Mont St. Michel. After so many months in the field, the flightsuits had become soiled and weathered, giving his team the appearance of a gang of drifters rather than a coordinated fighting unit. The addition of the winter gear Svetlana had gifted masked their haggard appearance. Most of his people were given the traditional Russian army winter coat with flora camouflage coloring and grey fur collars. The women were supplied with Soviet-era winter jackets designed for Afghanistan, which were tan with grey fur collars. Svetlana had saved the best for Jason—her grey wool overcoat with the black fur collar. He felt self-conscious in it because the coat made him stand out from the others; however, he would never have insulted Svetlana by refusing to accept it.

Sook-kyoung and Vicky unloaded the horses from the stock car, saddled them up, and brought them to where the others gathered around the steam engine. The Demon Hunters checked the packs and supplies. Jason had opted to travel only with the necessities. The minigun had been destroyed while closing the Irkutsk portal, so Jason assigned Haneef to carry one of the remaining antimatter devices; Ustagov and Sook-kyoung were responsible for the last two. Each device had been carefully packed to survive the rigors of the trip, being encased inside a pad of dark grey foam rubber two feet square that was then inserted into a saddle bag. Since Ustagov did not have a horse, he would use Neal's. Once Jason's team was ready, he pushed himself off the cowcatcher and made his way through the group, advising his people they should move out. As they mounted their horses, Jason walked over to Svetlana, who stood by the engineer's compartment.

She snapped at attention as he approached. "Is it time?"

"I'm afraid it is." Jason reached under his overcoat and unlatched the crossbow from his belt. He handed it to Svetlana.

"You won't need it?"

"I've been carrying it since Paris and have hardly used it. It's not very effective against ravagers and dragons. I want you to have it as a token of my appreciation."

Svetlana took the crossbow and examined it. "Once we get this world back into shape, the Russian people will write songs about you and the Demon Hunters."

Jason suppressed a groan of frustration at the thought of being immortalized in folk ballads, although it was a small price to pay for saving the world. He offered the colonel his hand. "Thank you for everything."

Instead of shaking it, Svetlana pulled Jason close, wrapped her arms around him, and kissed him on each cheek. When finished, she took his hands in her own and stepped back, letting their arms dangle between them. "You are a strong, decent man. Your mother would be proud."

Jason did not know how to respond.

Svetlana broke away, headed back to the train, and climbed up into the engineer's compartment. Jason returned to his team. Without saying a word, he mounted his horse and spurred it on. Lilith and Lucifer joined him on either side. The rest of his team followed.

Jason heard the steam engine's whistle blow. Looking over his shoulder, he watched as the train lurched and inched backward down the track, slowly gathering speed. Within a few minutes, the engine had traveled out of sight, with only a plume of thick black smoke marking its location. Jason felt a twinge of regret and apprehension. He was leaving behind new friends. He was also leaving behind the safety of the train and the firepower it provided. His team would never have made it this far without Svetlana. They were now on their own again. Even though Jason would never admit it to the others, he felt uncertain if they were up to the task. Months on the road had whittled their numbers, their strength, and their morale. With each portal being defended by an increasing number of demons, many more ferocious than those encountered before, the odds of success were turning against them.

Jason faced forward and led his team down the tracks. Harbin lay ahead of them.

Beyond that lay the unknown.

CHAPTER THREE

THE DEMON HUNTERS bunked down in an old warehouse along the train tracks on the southwest outskirts of Harbin. The building had two advantages. Not only was it large enough to comfortably house his team and their horses, it also stood isolated from the few buildings that surrounded it, making it impossible for anything to sneak up on them. Jason figured the latter would not be an issue. All afternoon, they had come across an abundance of wildlife, mostly deer, small animals, and a few cows and pigs, indicating the absence of predators. As the others gathered around the campfire and prepared dinner, Jason stood outside examining the city's skyline, which cast a dark shadow against the moonlit sky. From this distance, it appeared as a desolate landscape, with no lights or fires, no activity, and no signs of life, either human or demon.

Footsteps crunched against gravel. A moment later, Father Belsario stepped up beside him. "I hope I didn't startle you."

"If you were coming after me, I probably wouldn't have heard you until it was too late."

"Where are Lilith and Lucifer? They usually stick with you."

Jason gestured toward the warehouse. "They're hanging around the fire hoping to mooch some dinner. They have their priorities."

Father Belsario chuckled and then became serious again. "Matthew, Luther, and I are setting up the perimeter watch. Do you feel comfortable with having only three people, or do you want more?"

"I think three is okay per shift. I'll have my people relieve you at ten o'clock."

"That's not necessary. Remember, we don't need to rest as you do. We'll be fine until morning. Excuse me, please."

As the cleric walked off, Jason studied him. The Purgatoriati were an unusual and macabre addition to his team, yet one that had made the difference between life and death, success and failure. When the apocalypse began, Father Belsario had wanted to raise an army in Heaven to help Jason battle the Demon Spawn but could find no one willing to give up paradise, even temporarily. He then traveled to Purgatory to recruit, offering a commutation of banishment in exchange for service. Four men had volunteered—Gabriel, who had engaged in the slave trade until his own family was captured and sold, had died outside of Minsk; Jonah, who had renounced his religion to save his life when Jerusalem fell to the enemy during the Crusades, had died battling demons in Red Square; Luther, whose faith in science over religion had denied him salvation; and Matthew, the Knights Templar who had slaughtered innocents and died from typhus before he could atone for his sins. And, of course, Sasha, who had been drafted because, according to Father Belsario, she would play an important role in their future. When they had first met up with Jason's team outside of Minsk, no one had trusted them. That mistrust vanished after the first encounter with the Demon Spawn. The Purgatoriati fought with the same ferocity as the demons, and with their unlimited stamina took down as many of the creatures as the rest of the team combined. Since they were already dead, the Purgatoriati could not be killed in the traditional sense, so when one fell in combat, they would come back from Purgatory and rejoin the expedition. They had proved a Godsend to Jason because the Demon Hunters' numbers were dwindling rapidly.

Of the original twenty-one Demon Hunters who had set out for Paris to close the first portal, only seven had made it back to Mont St. Michel. Bolstered by four recruits, the team had then set out for Russia, losing another three of its members before closing the portals in Moscow and Siberia. The only reason the casualties remained so low was that the Russians and the Purgatoriati had joined their ranks, losing scores of their own soldiers and two Purgatoriati in the process. Now that his team was on its own again, Jason knew the death toll would climb significantly. If France was any indication of the losses they could suffer, he would be lucky to have anyone left by the time they reached the States.

Strolling back to the warehouse, Jason stopped at the entrance and watched the others around the campfire. Ian had found a dented cooking pot that he had cleaned up as best he could and hung over the flames to make dinner. Lucifer sat beside Ian, dutifully waiting for his turn to be fed. Lilith curled up beside Jeanette. Although he had barely known these people four months ago, the time spent on this journey had forged an unbreakable link between them. Jason considered them his family. To his surprise, the toughest part about going into combat was not battling Demon Spawn; it was watching his friends die. He had done too much of that lately. Sadly, he knew he would be experiencing it again.

Haneef, Slava, Antoine, and Sook-kyoung had been part of the group since the beginning, and Jeanette had joined them on the way to Paris. Haneef, quiet and pleasant, had been an exchange student from Sudan who had been caught in Paris when the portals opened. Slava was the opposite. A former street thug from Moscow, he fit the part: tall, muscular, spiked hair, and not very bright. Slava had proven himself to be an excellent fighter and fiercely loyal, which made him invaluable. Antoine had a background like Slava's. He had been an enforcer in a Moroccan gang in Chartres before the apocalypse, and eventually wound up at Mont St. Michel. Mean and violent on the battlefield, with his friends he remained self-effacing. Sook-kyoung had been in France as an exchange student from the University of Seoul when all Hell broke loose; although quiet and unassuming, she possessed a black belt in Taekwondo that made her as tough as the others. Jeanette had joined when the Demon Hunters were taken in by the Enclave, and she had agreed to lead them to the portal. She was roughly the same age as Jason and just as determined. Even the dirty, weathered flightsuit could not detract from her soft face, dimples, and long brunette hair. These five were his most trusted confidants as well as his fiercest fighters. They had witnessed horrors in Paris that the others in the group could barely imagine. That experience had changed them. It made them tough and determined, and it bonded them in a way only those who had undergone combat together could fully understand. Jason knew that any one of them would give their lives for him in a heartbeat, and he would do the same for them.

Ian, Gaston, and Vicky had been added prior to leaving for Moscow. An evolutionary biologist from Australia, Ian had asked to be part of what he viewed as a scientific expedition, and Jason had agreed because he felt Ian's expertise would come in handy, which it had. Gaston was slightly younger, in his mid-thirties, stout with scraggly dark hair. He had lost his farm when it had been overrun by Demon Spawn and wanted to join since he had nothing left. Jason brought him along for his survivalist skills. Vicky, the youngest member, not quite sixteen years old, had sad, dark brown eyes that mirrored all she had been through. She possessed no fighting skills, could barely handle a weapon, and had limited medical experience from working in her parents' apothecary. Jason had allowed her to join so she could escape a predatory situation back at Mont St. Michel. So far, Vicky had not disappointed him. None of the newcomers had let down the team, nor did he expect them to. However, the reality remained that these three were the least experienced, and as such were the most likely not to survive the next encounter with the demons, especially Vicky.

Slava waved for Jason to join them. As he approached, Jeanette slid over on the bench to make room.

"We need you to settle something for us," said the Russian.

Jason sat beside Jeanette. "What?"

"Ustagov thinks the Demon Spawn are developing the ability to think rationally."

"That's not what I said," the doctor protested. "I said I've noticed the Demon Spawn are starting to defend the portals, which will make our job that much harder."

"That implies they're smart enough to know we're attempting to close the portals," argued Slava.

"You're assuming—"

"The doctor's right," interrupted Jason. "The Demon Spawn have begun defending the portals."

An awkward silence fell across the group as everyone stared at Jason. Finally, Ian asked, "Are you serious, mate?"

"Unfortunately, I am. The one in Paris had been left wide open."

Antoine shook his head. "If you remember, we got slaughtered in Paris."

"Because we had to fight our way through the city. Once we got inside Notre Dame, nothing stood by the portal to protect it. The Russians told me that after they nuked the portal in Red Square, nothing but Flesh Eaters came through until we closed the one in Paris, and then the dragons emerged to guard it."

Ustagov snapped his fingers and pointed at Jason. "That's what I'm talking about."

Jason continued. "At Lake Baikal, three Golem blocked the tracks in front of the portal and tried to prevent us from reaching it. They would have derailed the engine if Sasha had not stayed with it and cleared the path with her minigun. The Demon Spawn realize we're closing the portals and intend to stop us."

"That doesn't make any sense," said Haneef. "Every demon we've encountered has shown no signs of intelligence beyond that of a wild animal. How can they know what we're trying to do let alone develop a game plan against us?"

"*They* can't," answered Vicky, who stared at the floor. "Something with higher intelligence is directing them."

"You can't be serious?" asked Slava.

"Why not?" Vicky lifted her head and met his gaze. "I was raised a strict Catholic and always had faith that Heaven and Hell were real. That's been proven, at least the Hell part. If we know there's a Heaven and angels because we know there's a Hell and demons, then if there's a God and saints—"

"Then there's also a Satan and anti-saints," concluded Sook-kyoung. "They're the ones directing the demons."

"Exactly," said Vicky.

Gaston sat forward and held up his hand. "Are you suggesting that Satan or someone else is behind all of this?"

Jason and Ustagov nodded.

Gaston leaned back, despair distorting his features. "I can't believe this is happening."

"What a surprise, huh, mate?" Ian leaned over and gently slugged the Frenchman in the shoulder. "Here we thought we were running around the world to close the doors so Hell's zoo wouldn't escape. Now we find out we're fighting off an invasion from the Underworld."

"Is that true?" Jeanette asked.

Ustagov shrugged. "There's no scientific evidence to suggest that Satan has launched an invasion. However, you can't dispute the fact that someone or something wants to keep the portals open."

"What about us?" Antoine asked. "Does this mean it's over?"

"Why would you ask that?"

"There's nine of us plus the Purgatoriati. There's no way we can pull this off if Hell is throwing everything it has against us."

Jason paused before answering. He felt everyone's eyes upon him, hoping for inspiration. As much as he wanted to say something that would rally his team, he did not lead that way. Honesty worked best, even if he told them what they did not want to hear.

"I'm not going to lie to you and say this'll be easy, or that some of us might get out of this alive. The chances are good we won't close all the portals. This is not what you signed up for, so I won't fault anyone who decides to call it quits and sets out on their own. You can take your horse, your weapon, and your share of the supplies, and I'll wish you the best. Before you make that decision, ask yourself if giving up now is worth it in the long run. All you'll be doing is buying some time. If even one of the portals remains open, it'll continue to pour demons into our realm. It may take years, but sooner or later they'll make their way to every corner of the globe, and humans will become extinct. It's a damned if you do and damned if you don't scenario, so if anyone wants to back out now, I understand, and no one will think any less of you."

"I'll think less of me," said Antoine. "I've been with you from the beginning, and I'll stay with you to the end."

"Thank you."

"Sorry for doubting you."

"No apologies necessary." Jason glanced at the others. "If there's anyone who would like to drop out, now's the time. I'm serious when I say there'll be no hard feelings."

Jeanette reached out and clasped his hand. "You know I'll stand by you."

"So will I," said Sook-kyoung.

"Maybe I'm insane," said Slava. "You've gotten us this far. If anyone can pull this off, it'll be you."

"It's Allah's will," added Haneef.

Vicky forced a grin. "Whatever the portal has to offer is better than what's waiting for me back home."

"I'm a survivalist," said Gaston. "This is the chance of a

lifetime, so of course I'm in."

"I'm in," said Ustagov. "I'd rather face a thousand ravagers than go back to Moscow and tell Colonel Krayevsky I left you."

Ian did not reply. Jason asked, "What about you?"

"Are you serious, mate?" Ian laughed. "When was the last time you heard of an Aussie backing down from a fight?"

"Thank you. I appreciate this." Jason pointed to the vat. "What's for dinner?"

"Ian's cooking," said Gaston. "So, you'll probably want to eat one of those Russian MREs."

"No, you wouldn't," said Slava. "They're as tough as shoe leather, only not as tasty."

"I'm a good cook, mate."

Gaston shrugged. "All I know is that since you've been cooking, we haven't run into any Demon Spawn."

Jason sniffed the vat. "Ian, what are you making?"

For a moment, Ian didn't answer. Finally, he mumbled, "I'm heating up some of the Russian MREs."

Gaston and Slava gave each other a high five as the others around the campfire chuckled.

"Piss off," said Ian as he suppressed his amusement.

"It could be worse," said Slava. "You know the old saying. The best army in the world is where the MPs are British, the mechanics are German, the chefs are Italian, and it's all organized by the Russians. The worst army is where the MPs are German, the mechanics are Russian, the chefs are British, and it is all organized by the Italians."

Everyone burst out laughing, except Antoine who looked back and forth at his friends. "I don't get it."

This made the others laugh harder. Even Antoine chuckled, although he was not certain why.

CHAPTER FOUR

T HE NIGHT PASSED uneventfully if somewhat restlessly. Jason wanted to give his team plenty of time to clear Harbin, so he woke everyone before dawn so they could eat and pack early. They set off shortly after sunrise. Jason and Father Belsario took the lead. Despite the latter's objections, Jason had insisted the cleric ride with him on one of the extra horses, refusing to have the leader of the Purgatoriati walk beside him. Father Belsario reluctantly agreed. Ustagov stayed close to the two men, navigating from the Russian-language map. Lilith and Lucifer plodded alongside their master, constantly alert for potential danger. The rest followed in single file at fifty-foot intervals. Everyone remained on edge, not knowing what dangers lay ahead. Other than a herd of deer grazing along the side of the tracks, they saw no signs of life.

A few hours later, they approached the Harbin city limits. A pair of chain link fences separated the tracks from the surrounding neighborhoods. After a few hundred feet, the fence became a retaining wall. A quarter of a mile ahead, the tracks disappeared into an underpass.

"Maybe we should go back," suggested Father Belsario.

"Why?"

"We're being funneled into a confined space. If the Demon Spawn attack us, we'll have nowhere to go."

"We don't have to worry about that," said Jason.

"How can you be sure?"

"I'm not sensing any presence. Not even a hum. There are no demons for miles around. I'm not even detecting humans."

Father Belsario cocked his head. "I didn't think you could detect human auras."

"I've been working on it. I'm able to sense benevolent presences, like the werehounds and your people, and can pick up severe emotional responses if they're close by."

"I hope you're certain about this."

"I am."

Shortly after, they reached Harbin West Railway Station. A single train sat on one of the lines. Jason led his horse up the ramp onto the platform. Scores of suitcases lay spread around, some tossed aside, while others had been opened and their contents rifled through. Smaller articles of clothing lay scattered around where gusts of wind had carried them. There were no signs of a panic or a struggle, no bodies or blood, no shattered glass or debris. Reaching the stairs in the center of the platform, Jason and his team maneuvered their horses up the handicap access ramp to the terminal. Here they found a similar scene. Suitcases littered the floor of the cavernous waiting hall, many opened and rummaged through. The only signs of complete chaos were at the food stalls along either wall. Refrigerators and food dispensers had been cleaned out. Containers, cups, napkins, utensils, and anything not edible covered the floors.

Ustagov brought his horse alongside Jason. "The last train out of Harbin never left, so everyone took what they could and set out on their own."

"To where?" asked Father Belsario.

Crossing the terminal, Jason led his team out into the courtyard in front of the station and stopped by the handicap access ramp leading to the lower level and the Xinhua International Shopping Center. He motioned for Ustagov to join him.

"What's up?"

"Where do we go from here?"

The doctor unzipped his winter coat, slid out the map from

the inner pocket, and studied it. He pointed south to a large thoroughfare. "That's Zhongxing Street. It'll take us to the main road to Shenyang."

"Then let's move out." Jason maneuvered his horse to face the rest of his team. "I'm not sensing any Demon Spawn in the area, or anything that could pose a threat. There still could be packs of wild animals, so stay alert."

Jason exited the courtyard, proceeded down Xizhan Street, and veered left onto Zhongxing Street. As the team made its way through the banking district, Jason silently studied the surroundings. Other than assorted small wildlife and the occasional stray cat or dog, he detected no indications of life in the city. In fact, nothing had lived here for months. Litter blew through the gutters. Several cars and trucks had been abandoned, most pushed against the sidewalks, a few left in the middle of the road. A bus with a flat tire sat at an angle against the curb, with discarded luggage around it like at the train station. Farther ahead, they passed a block lined with shops. Even here the chaos appeared minimal. Clothing and electronic stores remained as they did the day their owners locked the doors. Only the food and drug stores had been looted, people taking the necessities to survive. In many places, nature had begun to reclaim civilization. Cracks along the streets and sidewalks brimmed with grass and saplings, as did windowsills and flat roofs. Everything not overrun was coated with a thick layer of dirt and dust.

Harbin reminded him of so many of the smaller cities and towns they had encountered in France and Russia that had not been destroyed or ravaged by Demon Spawn, but merely had been evacuated before the flood of demonic hordes. The world had been shattered, and the opening of the interdimensional portals had disrupted billions of lives. How many people died as the demons spread across the globe, and how many died from disease or starvation in the ensuing months? How many were still alive? How many would be alive when they closed the last portal, if the team made it that far?

Sadness tinged Jason's soul when he thought about this being his mother's legacy.

Dr. Lisa McCreary had been the driving force behind Project Discovery, the joint attempt with hadron colliders in Russia, China, Japan, and the United States to generate more antimatter at one time than had been attempted before. She had described the project as an effort to advance the field of science significantly; in truth, she had ignored those who had warned against the possible consequences, hoping to make a name for herself in the scientific community. In that she succeeded, although not in the manner she had hoped. The generation of so much anti-matter at once created an electromagnetic pulse that destroyed the world's electronics in a matter of seconds and destabilized the borders between Earth and Hell, opening portals connecting the two. Each supercollider created a one-way entry portal into Hell while simultaneously punching out a one-way exit portal at another location. The latter were the most dangerous because they allowed hordes of Demon Spawn to spill out and spread across this realm. Until the portals were closed, the planet faced the possibility of being overrun by demons.

The entry portals concerned Jason for only one reason— the one at CERN in Geneva had sucked his mother into Hell.

At first, Jason had taken on his mother's guilt for opening the portals and allowed it to consume him. He saw his chance for redemption when his friend Doc developed anti-matter devices, football-sized steel containers containing frozen particles of anti-matter that, when thrown through an exit portal, would interact with the matter in the portal and snuff it out. Jason agreed to accompany the team that would test the device on the portal in Paris, hoping that by doing so it would clear his name. In time, Jason realized his motivations were wrong. He did not have to clear his name because he had done nothing to tarnish it. Nor could he clear his mother's name because her vanity and arrogance had resulted in the apocalypse, and nothing anyone could do could erase that sin. After their initial success in Paris, Jason organized this expedition to close the remaining portals because it was the right thing to do. He had a chance, as slim as it might be, to restore the world to some semblance of order. Jason could not live with himself knowing he enjoyed a demon-free France while the rest of the world was ravaged. Only time would tell if he would fail or succeed, or if he would die trying. In any case, he woke every morning with a clear conscience.

However, even though Jason's mother bore the responsibility for what had happened, that did not mean he planned to abandon her to the Underworld. Jason had contemplated this decision since closing the portal in Notre Dame and cutting off his mother's attempt to escape. He had suppressed his guilt by rationalizing that there had been no other options, yet privately, for weeks afterward, Jason had questioned his reasoning. Was being trapped in Hell his mother's punishment for the destruction she had caused? Was this divine retribution for her sin, or a Faustian price she needed to pay for her arrogance? In any case, it did not matter. She may have caused the apocalypse, but she was still his mother. Once Jason had saved the world, he hoped to save her as well. He only had to figure out how.

After traveling three miles, Ustagov raced up beside Jason. He held the map in his lap, balancing it on his knee with his right hand. "Zhengyi Road is up ahead. If we take that south, it'll put us on the main road to Shenyang."

"You're sure about that?"

The doctor nodded. "Once we get on that road, it'll be clear sailing all the way."

"I doubt it'll be clear sailing," said Jason.

"What about it, Father?" Ustagov asked. "Maybe you could pray for it."

Father Belsario shook his head. "It doesn't work that way,

my son. God gives guidance to the faithful. He doesn't interfere in the affairs of man."

"Sort of like 'hope for the best and prepare for the worst'?" asked Jason.

"Precisely."

"That's how I've lived for the past year. Let's hope it continues to work."

At the intersection with Zhengyi Road, Jason turned right and led the team south. With luck, it would take a few weeks to find and close the portal. He hoped they would be able to travel for a while before being detected.

FROM HIS POSITION on the top floor of the China Construction Bank's office building, Deng watched through his binoculars as the horsemen exited the train station and proceeded down Zhongxing Street. He counted eleven people on horseback and two on foot, plus two large dogs. Except for one young woman, none of them were Asian. He found their presence unusual since no one had ventured into this region since the arrival of Bai three months ago. Even more bizarre, he had not seen Westerners since the *shìjiè mòrì*, or what the West referred to as the End of Days. Deng wondered if these were the ones the stories talked about, the travelers with the ability to deny Hell access to this world. It didn't matter. Qiang wanted to be warned of any outsiders who entered the area; it was why he had posted lookouts in abandoned towns and cities throughout the province.

Deng observed the outsiders as they made their way along Zhongxing Street. The group did not set up camp, search for survivors, or loot what few supplies remained. They seemed interested only in passing through, which was confirmed when the horses turned onto one of the major roads leading toward Shenyang.

31

When the last of the outsiders were no longer in sight, Deng raced down the stairwell to the bank's lobby where he had hidden his bicycle. Walking it out onto the sidewalk, he checked one final time to make sure the outsiders had not backtracked. Mounting the bicycle, he followed their path along Zhongxing Street and turned right onto Xuefu Road, which paralleled Zhengyi Road. Deng pedaled as fast as he could, hoping to put distance between him and the outsiders and to warn Qiang in plenty of time to prepare for them.

CHAPTER FIVE

THE TEAM STOPPED ten miles south of Harbin where Zhengyi Road came to an end. As the others milled around, stretching or wandering to a secluded area to relieve themselves, Jason and Father Belsario glared disapprovingly at Ustagov. The doctor held the map spread out on top of a mailbox as he studied it.

"Just admit we're lost," said Jason after several minutes.

"I never said we weren't. We're not that far off course." Ustagov tapped his finger on the map and waved over Jason and Father Belsario.

"Here's the problem. Back in Harbin, we should have taken Xuefu Road, which was two streets over. That would have led us to the G1, which will take us directly to Shenyang. If we follow the road we're on for three miles, it'll take us to the G1."

"Are you sure?" Father Belsario had a tone of skepticism in his voice. "Back in Harbin, you told us this was the right road."

"I know how to read a map," snapped Ustagov. "I'm not used to reading one from a moving horse."

"Fair enough," said Jason, wanting to end any arguments. "No harm done."

"Thank you." The doctor nodded. "We can reach the G1 by nightfall."

"It's two hours until sunset. I'd rather find a secure place for the night."

JASON SELECTED A spot only a few blocks away among the remnants of an old factory that stood three stories tall. A portion of one wall and two of the three smokestacks towered into the sky; the middle stack had collapsed. Segments of the cement foundation outlined the structure's original location. It offered enough open space to stable the horses and be easily defendable while the wall protected them from the cold. By the time night fell, the camp had been set up, and the team warmed themselves in front of the open flames.

Tonight's meal consisted of another round of Russian MREs. As the others finished eating, Father Belsario crouched down to chat with Jason. "Matthew, Luther, and I will take watch again tonight."

"Thanks. After dinner, I'm going to have my people join you."

"There's no need for that. We'll wake you if something happens."

"I don't want my people becoming complacent by not standing watch. Besides, we should beef up the guard a bit." Jason lowered his voice. "I sense something unusual out there."

"Demon Spawn?"

"Nothing we've encountered before, but I'd rather err on the side of caution than have the whole thing end here."

"I agree."

"Do you know when the rest of your people will rejoin us?"

"I don't. It's been three weeks since Gabriel died, and almost a week since we lost Jonah and Sasha. I assumed they'd be back by now. This is all new to me."

"I understand." Jason was not entirely sure he did, though. "I'll have my people man the watch after dinner."

Father Belsario stood and wandered off to set up the perimeter guard.

"I'm not worried," said Ian. "Between your ability to detect those things and the thick walls of this factory, we'll be safe."

Ustagov chuckled.

"What's so funny, mate?"

"This isn't a factory," the doctor replied. "It's the remains of the crematorium for Unit 731."

"What's that?" asked Antoine.

"When the Japanese occupied northern China during World War II, they set up a secret biological warfare research facility outside of Harbin." Ustagov pointed to the wall behind him. "The main facility stood a few hundred yards in that direction. Today it's an elementary school."

"Are you kidding?" asked Vicky.

Ustagov shook his head. "The Japanese developed plague, smallpox, and cholera and tested their effectiveness on local villages. They would infect people with diseases and dissect them alive to document how the pathogens affected the body. Some of the experiments the Japanese conducted here rivaled what the Nazis were doing in Germany. Most of the victims were Chinese, but a lot were Korean, Russian, and even Allied POWs. Two hundred and fifty thousand people were murdered. Most of the bodies were disposed of right here."

"How do you know all this?" asked Sook-kyoung.

"I took a course on biological warfare at university," answered Ustagov. "We spent a week on Unit 731. Once you know what went on here, you can never forget it. It's sad, we've been so distracted by the chaos the Demon Spawn have caused we sometimes forget that man can be just as brutal to each other."

Haneef said to Jason, "That would explain the bad vibes you've been feeling."

Jason hoped not. If he had the ability to sense the souls of those who met a violent end, then every person who had died because of the Demon Spawn would weigh down on him, and he did not think he could handle that.

"That's enough cheery talk for tonight." Jason stood and tossed his empty MRE pouch into the fire. "Gaston, Ian, Vicky. I want you to stand watch with the Purgatoriati until eleven. Antoine, Sook-kyoung, and Jeanette will relieve you at 0300. Slava, Haneef, and I will take over from then until morning. Get a good night sleep, everyone. I want to be on the road right after sunrise."

As the others packed up and prepared to go about their business, Jason stepped away from the campfire and crossed the foundation of the former crematorium, wanting to clear his mind of what Ustagov had told them. Lilith and Lucifer trotted along beside him. He had walked only a few hundred feet when he heard Jeanette call after him.

"Jason, wait."

He stopped. "What's up?"

"Ever since we left the train you've been pushing the group."

"So?"

"Why are you so anxious to keep moving? We have a long trip ahead of us. If you keep driving us at this rate, we'll burn out before we finish what we've set out to do."

"It's a risk I have to take," Jason answered. "If the doctor and I are right and the Demon Spawn are protecting the portals, it makes sense to close them as quickly as possible before they build up their defenses to the point we can't get past them. I know the pace I'm asking us to maintain is tough, but it's better than having to fight against heavily-fortified portals."

"Are you sure that's the only reason?"

"What are you talking about?"

Jeanette's tone became icy. "You're in a hurry to get back to Sasha."

The statement caught Jason off guard. "Why do you say that?"

"You asked Father Belsario about her."

"I asked about all the Purgatoriati. Not having them here puts a strain on our ability to fight the demons. And it doesn't matter how fast we travel. When Sasha and the others return, they'll track us down like they did outside of Minsk. I'm in a hurry so we can finish this as soon as possible. Now if you'll excuse me."

Jason walked away, but Jeanette circled around and cut him off. "I'm afraid I'm losing you to Sasha."

"Why would you think that?"

"Why did you want her fighting beside you to deploy the device at Lake Baikal?"

"Because she's one of the best fighters I've ever known—"

"You don't think I'm tough?"

"And," continued Jason, "Sasha knew how to use the minigun. Besides, if something happened to her, she'd come back from the dead. You wouldn't."

"If I did come back from Purgatory, would you react to me the same way you did when she joined us outside of Minsk."

"What do you expect? I was thrilled to see her again. I thought I'd lost her forever."

"That's what I mean."

"This is ridiculous." Jason tried to go around Jeanette. She stepped in front of him again.

"Admit you still love Sasha."

"I've never denied it. She's my best friend."

"But you wish you were more than friends."

Jason had become irritated by this conversation. "Yes, when I first met Sasha, I fell in love with her and wanted us to be together. That never happened. She kept on ignoring me. Then I met and fell in love with you."

"Do you mean that?"

"Of course."

Jeanette clasped his hands and moved closer. "Then let's sleep together."

"When?"

"What's wrong with right now?

The conversation, like Jason's frustration, was getting out of hand. He needed to take control of the situation. "Jeanette, I love you and—"

She released his hands and took a step back. "I'm not convinced you do."

Jason had no idea how to respond.

Jeanette sighed and lowered her head. "I came on this expedition partly because I believed in the cause and partly because I thought you cared about me as much as I do about you. Obviously, I was wrong. I can live with it. But I can't help feeling that you're not completely honest with—"

Jason winced. His sixth sense activated, although not because it had detected Demon Spawn. The sensation hit him unexpectedly. He was familiar with the vibe and did not feel threatened by it.

Father Belsario rushed up. "Something's approaching from the west."

"I know," said Jason reassuringly. "It's nothing to be concerned about."

Three large shadows approached, their forms creating vague outlines in the dark. As they moved closer, it became apparent their cloaks generated the shadows. Each figure rode a horse. Two empty horses brought up the rear, their bridles linked to the saddles in front of them by rope. Light from the campfire illuminated the emblems emblazoned into their breastplates, a circle surrounding a raised R in the upper left quadrant and a raised A in the lower right, with a brass crucifix centered between the letters. Jason felt a twinge of happiness and relief when he spotted the tints of auburn hair.

Sasha stopped her horse in front of Jason and smiled. "Are we interrupting anything?"

CHAPTER SIX

J ASON CLOSED THE distance with Sasha as she dismounted. He hugged her, even though he knew the gesture would piss off Jeanette. She spun around with a huff and stormed off.

Sasha broke the hug and watched Jeanette leave. "Is everything okay?"

"Nothing you need to be concerned about."

Father Belsario greeted Gabriel and Jonah as they slid out of their saddles, blessing each with the sign of the cross, and then did the same to Sasha. "We're glad you're back. Jason and I were worried you wouldn't be joining us."

Gabriel snorted. "I wish."

Jonah nodded.

Sasha rolled her eyes. "It was made quite clear to us that we still have plenty of work to do down here before our time in Purgatory can be shortened."

"Were the horses sent with you?" asked Jason.

Jonah shook his head. "We returned near an abandoned horse farm. These guys were wandering the fields eating grass. We found some saddles and bridles, geared them up, and brought them with us. It beats walking everywhere."

"Plus, they can help us carry supplies," added Gabriel.

"Good thinking," said Father Belsario.

"Yes." Jason suddenly became excited. "Do you know where to find the portal?"

Gabriel and Jonah shook their heads. Sasha frowned. "We materialized a few miles west of here and sensed the rest of the group in this direction."

"I was afraid of that." Father Belsario shrugged. "It's part of Heaven's no interference on Earth policy."

"Somebody should tell Hell they need to adopt the same standards," said Jonah.

Jason headed back to the campfire and motioned for the others to follow.

"We have to stand watch," said Father Belsario. "Do you still have that unusual sensation you picked up on earlier?"

Jason shook his head.

"Then you probably felt their presence. I don't think there's any need for your people to stand watch with us."

"I still want them to," said Jason.

"Fair enough."

As the Purgatoriati moved off to take up their positions, Jason reached out for Sasha. "At least say hello to everyone. They'll be glad you're back."

Sasha hesitated. Father Belsario flashed her a disapproving glare. "I can't right now."

"Okay." Jason made no attempt to hide his disappointment.

Father Belsario headed back to his position. Jonah and Gabriel joined him. Sasha followed, paused for a moment to let the others get ahead of her, and dashed over to Jason. She hugged him and gently kissed his cheek. "We'll talk later."

Jason stayed until Sasha had disappeared into the night before heading back to the others.

"THREE MORE JUST joined the group." Deng peered through his binoculars.

"I don't like this," added Min, Qiang's deputy.

Deng lowered the binoculars. "You don't think these are the travelers everyone is talking about, do you?"

Qiang said nothing. Deng had arrived at the forward recon

post this afternoon and reported the outsider's presence. Qiang and Min accompanied him to track them down. They had traveled through Pinfang because the town connected with Zhengyi Road. Qiang hoped to circle around behind the outsiders and follow them. He and his men would have walked right into their camp if the latter had not built such a large fire. Retreating far enough away so their horses could not be heard, they tied up the animals and backtracked, finding a spot where no one would discover them.

Qiang studied the outsiders through a second set of binoculars, analyzing their behavior. They did not appear threatening. However, since the End of Days he had learned the hard way that looks could be deceiving. He refused to believe the stories of a group of wanderers traveling the globe slaughtering demons and denying Hell access to this world; just as he refused to accept the stories about a large portion of the United States having survived and getting ready to fight back. These were fantasies created to bolster the people's spirits in dark times. Despite the coincidence of these outsiders showing up shortly after the rumors began circulating, Qiang attributed no significance to their presence. He hoped they were merely refugees escaping from some unspeakable horror to the west, and not fanatics coming here to seek salvation. He had enough to do dealing with the Sataners.

"How do you want to handle this?" asked Min.

"For now, we wait and watch." Qiang lowered his binoculars. "With luck, they're just passing through."

"What if they're not?"

"In that case, if whatever they intend to do is counter to our plans, we'll have to eliminate them."

CHAPTER SEVEN

THE TEAM SET out shortly after sunrise, continuing south along the G1. Except for Father Belsario, who rode beside Jason, the rest of the Purgatoriati gathered in a small cluster at the center of the group, chatting with their comrades who had arrived last night. Figuring he would never get a better opportunity, Ustagov dropped away from the lead and slowed his pace until the Purgatoriati caught up with him. He maneuvered his horse beside them.

"Good morning."

"Morning," Sasha replied. The others stared at the doctor warily.

"Can we chat?"

Matthew creased his eyebrows. "You realize we're not much into conversation?"

"I know you keep to yourselves. It's your thing. I get that. I'm dying to know about the Purgatoriati in general and each of you in particular."

"The doctor wasn't part of the group when we first joined them," explained Sasha. "You want to know our backstories, am I right?"

"Exactly," Ustagov blurted out.

"Why are you so interested?" Matthew asked.

"Call it scientific curiosity."

"There's nothing scientific about it," said Luther. "Our being here is a matter of faith.

"Several thousand years ago, before recorded history, God and Satan agreed not to interfere on Earth and to allow humans to use free will to choose between good or evil. Even though Satan had nothing to do with the opening of the portals, he's exploiting the situation to take over the Earth. God decided to raise a legion to fight the demons, but no one in Heaven wanted to leave Paradise. Father Belsario could only find volunteers in Purgatory. By fighting the Demon Spawn, we each get five hundred years taken off our banishment. That's why we have the R and A on our chest plates. They stand for Repentance and Atonement. Father Belsario only chose those who were truly repentant of their sins."

"What sins did you commit?" Ustagov immediately regretted his question. "I'm sorry. I shouldn't have asked. It's probably too personal."

"It is," said Jonah, his boyish features becoming solemn. "Part of our atonement is admitting what we have done. I was a young man when Jerusalem fell during the Crusades. Terrified of being tortured and executed, I renounced my faith and denounced my god to stay alive."

"God punished you for being afraid?" Ustagov asked.

"My god punished me for my betrayal. Faith in my true religion would have earned me an eternal afterlife. I forfeited that for a few extra years on Earth."

Matthew spoke next, his expression stoic under his red beard. "I was a Knights Templar in the Holy Land. Although I thought I had been devoting my life to fulfilling God's will, only later did I realize I had sinned by killing innocents in His name. I left the order and spent what little remained of my life in the Holy Land preaching the true word of Jesus. I died two years later of typhus. The renunciation of my previous life kept me out of Hell. However, by the time of my death I had not performed enough good deeds to atone for the sins I had committed. That's why I'm here."

Ustagov turned to Gabriel. "How did you end up in Purgatory?"

Gabriel stared straight ahead. "Slavery."

"You were a slave?"

"A trader." Gabriel faced the doctor. As he did, his black ponytail slid over his shoulder and dropped down his back. "Back then it was a perfectly acceptable profession, at least in the eyes of man. My religion considered those of other faiths who were conquered as the spoils of war. I sold women and young girls into the sex trade and men and boys into hard labor. I made a good living at it, so much so that I settled down, built a home, and started my own family."

"What happened?"

"My family was traveling to visit my mother when raiders attacked their caravan. They sold my wife into prostitution, made my daughter the concubine of the raider commander, and executed my son for defending the honor of his mother and sister. Only then did I realize the depravity of the sins I had committed; however, my regret came too late to save myself."

"I'm sorry," said Ustagov.

"I'm the one who's sorry, sorry for all the heartache and suffering I caused. You claim to be a man of science, doctor. I used to consider myself a man of business as well as a man of faith. Trust me when I say our faith and our beliefs mean nothing. It's our actions that count. I didn't realize that and suffered dearly for it on Earth and in Purgatory. I now have a chance to perform actions that can redeem my soul, and I intend to do that."

For a moment, Ustagov said nothing. He focused on Luther. "I'm afraid to ask about your sin."

"You should be." Luther's blue eyes expressed more irony than humor. "My sin is much like yours. I wound up in Purgatory because I accepted science as my religion, in my case medicine. I shunned religion from the moment I entered university in 18th Century Nuremberg, writing it off as a salve for those weak of mind and spirit, a way for the church to control the people during their miserable lives. I wanted to make a difference, so I spent my life discovering the causes of diseases and curing the sick, especially amongst the poor. My good deeds kept me out of Hell while my lack of faith kept me out of Heaven. You should consider my story a cautionary tale."

Ustagov changed the topic. "What about you, Sasha?"

Sasha sighed. "I have no idea why I was banished or why I was chosen to be part of the Purgatoriati. No one ever explained to me my sins. After I fell off the bell tower at Notre Dame, I woke up in Purgatory where Father Belsario drafted me. He keeps saying there's a special reason I'm here but won't tell me what it is."

Ustagov did not press the issue, knowing that Sasha's presence caused a rift between Jason and Jeanette. "What about Father Belsario? What sins did he commit?"

"None," said Luther. "When God couldn't get anyone in Heaven to come back to Earth, Father Belsario volunteered to go to Purgatory to raise recruits."

"That's dedication."

Luther raised an eyebrow. "That, my dear doctor, is faith."

"When you came back you received superhuman powers?" asked Ustagov.

Luther shook his head. "The Purgatoriati have been granted increased strength and agility, though nothing you could term superhuman. We don't need sleep and we don't get tired. In battle, we have the strength of five men. While we feel pain the way you do, it doesn't impair our ability to fight. Minor wounds heal quickly. If our bodies are destroyed or take enough damage to be rendered useless, our souls are transported back to Purgatory, and then we're resurrected a few days later."

"Amazing," Ustagov said under his breath.

"What is?" asked Jonah.

"That the existence of Heaven and Hell is a reality and no longer just a matter of faith. Two years ago, I scoffed at the idea. Now that their existence is empirically proven I have no choice but to accept."

"Are you now a man of faith?" Luther asked.

Ustagov chuckled. "My parents were devoted members of the Communist Party, and I received my training as a scientist in the former Soviet Union. Faith is not something that comes naturally to a man like me."

"I can empathize with your situation," said Luther. "On the bright side, if you die out here, maybe you'll be banished to Purgatory like me and can come back as one of us."

Ustagov nodded. The prospect of death scared him, although not as much as coming back as one of the Purgatoriati.

FOR LUTHER, THE discussion with Ustagov had generated his own set of questions. When the doctor returned to the front of the column, Luther caught Matthew's attention and motioned for his comrade to join him. Together, the two slowed their pace and dropped back until they were parallel with Jonah and Gabriel.

Gabriel eyed them suspiciously. "What's going on?"

"I'm curious about something," said Luther. "What happened after you guys died in Russia?"

"The same thing that happened when we first died," Gabriel replied. "We woke up in Purgatory."

"Did anyone greet you?"

"Someone met me," said Jonah. "Sister Francesca. She guided me through the process while I waited for my time to come back."

"Sister Francesca did the same for me," added Gabriel. "She didn't show up until after I had been there for a few days."

"What was she doing there?" Matthew asked.

Jonah chuckled. "Like Father Belsario, she wasn't easy to

get to know. I'd mentioned to Sister Francesca one night we were losing so many people closing the portals that I wondered if we were truly contributing to saving Earth. She told me she had been a Catholic nun in Lyons during World War II and had been tortured and murdered by the Gestapo for helping the French Resistance. Then she chastised me, reminding me that small acts of courage build up over time and can defeat even the greatest evil and that I should put my faith in God and think more positively."

Gabriel nodded, himself having experienced her charms.

"Is she recruiting others to join us?" asked Luther.

Jonah shook his head. "I asked Sister Francesca that. She became even more stern than usual and told me to concentrate on doing my best for the Purgatoriati. Any time I tried to bring up the subject with others, they either had no idea what I was talking about or would curtly end the topic."

"There's no indication that anyone in Purgatory is being recruited to join us," added Gabriel. "I got the feeling that the six of us are going to be constantly recycled through the system until we close all the portals. And no one wants to admit that out of fear we'll refuse to continue and opt to serve out our term in Purgatory."

"Maybe we're an embarrassment," said Luther.

"You don't think we're doing a good job?" Matthew huffed.

"I'm not referring to our performance, but to our very existence." Luther lowered his voice. "Remember, no one in Heaven wanted to fight the Demon Spawn, so Father Belsario had to find recruits in Purgatory. We've more than exceeded their expectations. And three of us have died a second time. Heaven may be afraid to recruit any more of us because it'll expose the hypocrisy of the faithful."

"Don't talk like that." Jonah said it more as a warning than out of anger. "You got yourself in trouble in your first life thinking that way."

"Don't worry. I'm one of the faithful now and don't mind atoning for my past sins. You must admit though, all the secrecy is unsettling. It's almost as if they're refusing to tell us we're the only ones who are Purgatoriati because they're afraid we won't come back next time."

Gabriel and Jonah protested that. Matthew lowered his head. "I confess I've had second thoughts."

The others stared at him.

"We can be wounded in combat and die a painful death." Matthew focused on Gabriel and Jonah. "You missed the battle at Lake Baikal. It was far more brutal than Minsk or Moscow. And the battles are only going to get tougher as the Demon Spawn fight harder to keep the portals open. How many times are we going to die violently and come back, only to die again?"

None of the others responded. Their facial expressions indicated that they had at least contemplated the idea.

Luther broke the silence. "How does Sasha feel about this?"

Gabriel frowned. "They've kept her even more in the dark about what's going on than they have us, though she'll come back no matter how many times she dies. She's still in love with Jason."

"I feel bad for her," said Jonah.

"Why?"

"She doesn't mind being part of the Purgatoriati because she's able to be with Jason. Once we close the portals, she'll be devastated."

CHAPTER EIGHT

BAI RESTED IN an old recliner salvaged from a house whose occupants had fled and left the doors open. The dark cloak draped over her body and covered the weathered upholstery. Mei sat at her feet, listening intently as Bai related stories of the Promised Land and the new beginning that awaited them all. Mei found such tales rapturous. After so many decades of suffering under Communism and so much horror following Armageddon, it brought comfort to know that a better future lay in store for humanity. A future Mei was helping to bring about.

A noise outside their tent distracted Mei. She snapped her head around in irritation, ready to scold the transgressor who had interrupted such a peaceful moment. The bad karma dissipated as rapidly as it had formed. Negativity had no place in this new world. Mei mentally asked for forgiveness and waited. A few moments later, one of the scouts burst through the tent flaps. Upon spotting Bai, he bowed his head and fell to one knee, cupping one hand over the other.

"Pardon the intrusion, Mistress."

Bai nodded slightly.

"I should have knocked first."

"Yes, you should have." Mei softened the harshness of her tone. "I trust there is a reason for your enthusiasm."

"There is." The scout did not budge.

"What is so important?" asked Bai.

Having received the Mistress' approval, the scout rose and nodded to the two women. "We've found the travelers you prophesized about."

"Where?" Mei's tone rose in excitement.

"My team observed them heading south on the G1, approximately twenty miles from Harbin."

"How many are there?"

"Fifteen. They're on horseback and headed for Shenyang."

Bai sat forward in the recliner. "Have the Unbelievers found them?"

The scout averted his gaze. "I'm afraid so, Mistress. We detected a few of them trailing the travelers, keeping their distance and watching them. As of when I left to report to you, the Unbelievers had not made contact."

Mei became agitated. "We can't let that happen."

"It won't." The scout again made eye contact with the women. "I told the rest of my team to continue tracking the travelers and to keep their distance, but, if the Unbelievers attempted to make contact, stop them. I hope I did not overstep my boundaries."

Mei strolled over and placed a reassuring hand on his shoulder. "You did the right thing. Thank you."

"We must not let the Unbelievers get to the travelers before we do," said Bai in her mesmerizing yet unsettling voice.

"I'll make certain of that, Mistress. You can rely on me."

"I know I can." Bai leaned back in her chair and rested.

Mei ushered the scout outside. "Go back to your team and continue what you're doing. Send someone here to report every morning, or if they change course."

"Of course, ma'am." The scout raced off.

Mei could not believe how events were playing out. Bai had predicted the arrival of the travelers and, even though many doubted her words, they had shown up. Plans had already been developed for this and any contingency resulting from their arrival. The camp would be broken down within an hour and would head north. Mei needed to meet the travelers and let events take their course for the glory of the Promised Land.

CHAPTER NINE

THE NEXT THREE days passed slowly and without incident, which Jason appreciated. All along the G1, they witnessed the aftermath of the devastating EMP. Thousands of vehicles had been left along the highway, each where they were driving when the pulse hit. Most had their doors and trunks open and had been rummaged through, either by the owners taking items of value or by survivors searching for anything salvageable. On the second day, they had come upon an electric train half a mile distant that had stopped on the tracks. Jason did not bother checking it out for he knew it had been ransacked long ago. Occasionally, they came upon a partially-clothed skeleton either seated in a vehicle or collapsed on the highway, the person it belonged to having died and been picked clean by animals.

What Jason did not see were signs that the Demon Spawn had made it this far north. Not that he had a desire to waste any of his resources battling all the way to Shenyang, but after almost a year of the portals being open, he anticipated some demons should have wandered this far. The flesh eaters from Paris had made it as far as Normandy, and those from Moscow had traveled as far as Minsk, yet his team had yet to come across anything unusual. Jason had not even detected a hum of a demonic presence since arriving in Harbin. The lack of Demon Spawn bothered him. The fact they had not traveled this far north made him wonder if the portal was near Shenyang. No one had confirmed its location. For all he knew, it could be hundreds of miles away in Shanghai or Shenzhen. He prayed he wasn't leading his team on a wild goose chase that would waste time and, most probably, lives while the portal sat somewhere else, spewing forth demons.

On the fourth night out of Harbin, they established camp at a small village along the banks of the Songhua River halfway to Changchun. There were only two dozen houses in town, so Jason picked one with a fenced in yard where the horses could graze. Sook-kyoung and Vicky made certain the animals were settled while the others set up in the accompanying residence. Ian discovered a bag of rice and a box of noodles hidden away in the top cupboard of the kitchen, which meant tonight they were spared another round of Russian MREs. The Purgatoriati joined them, for conversation rather than food, which over time solidified the bond between the two groups. Jason appreciated that, both for the camaraderie it generated and because it kept him from having to discuss difficult topics. Jeanette had barely spoken to him since their argument three nights ago and, when she did, she acted cold and angry. Nor had he a chance to speak with Sasha about what had happened at Lake Baikal because Father Belsario always intervened, like an overprotective father trying to keep his daughter away from the kid with the bad reputation. Jason reasoned that if he could not talk to Jeanette or Sasha, at least he avoided uncomfortable conversations.

Ian ruined that.

"Am I the only one who finds it odd that we've been heading for Shenyang for four days and have yet to come across any Demon Spawn?"

"I've been thinking the same thing," said Ustagov. "Flesh eaters spread for hundreds of miles from the portal in Moscow, yet we haven't spotted a single one."

"We haven't even come across a grumpy panda," added Slava, earning some subdued laughs from the group.

"What gives?" Antoine asked.

Father Belsario's features crinkled into his usual frown.

"We have to consider the possibility that we're nowhere near the portal."

The others stared at him, their eyes ranging from surprise to disbelief to anger.

"You can't be serious," said Vicky. "You mean we've come all this way for nothing?"

Father Belsario began to speak when Jason cut in. "He didn't say we've come all this way for nothing. He said we must consider the possibility that the portal isn't nearby. Svetlana said rumors *reported* it to be somewhere between Harbin and Shenyang."

Ustagov shrugged. "That's true. We've been operating on an assumption."

"We also have to consider that the portal might not be in China at all," Jason added. Several of his team began talking at once. He held up his hand to stop them. "We'll keep heading south until we either stumble upon the portal or find someone who can give us more accurate intelligence."

Sasha tried to change the mood. "We must be on the right track. Why would this whole region be abandoned if there wasn't something nearby the locals wanted to get away from?"

"Maybe there's something out there more dangerous than Demon Spawn," replied Antoine.

Jason felt the group's mood drop.

"Let's change the subject." Ustagov leaned toward Sasha. "I have a question I've been anxious to ask, although it might be inappropriate."

"Then maybe you shouldn't ask it," warned Father Belsario in a stern voice.

The doctor either did not hear or ignored the cleric. "From a scientific perspective, I'd like to know what you experienced back at Lake Baikal when you passed through the portal."

Sasha lowered her gaze.

"I shouldn't have asked," said Ustagov. "You don't have to answer."

"I don't mind." Sasha lifted her head. Her eyes were cold and distant. "I never felt anything so excruciating, and I fell to my death from the bell tower of Notre Dame. Because of the train's speed, it happened instantaneously; for me it felt like seconds. I didn't pass through the portal. I disintegrated against it. Or crumbled, or broke apart... I'm not sure how to describe it. Everything that touched the surface ceased to exist. I felt it first in my hands and arms. They seared away. I cried out from the agony, then my mouth and face were gone. I remember mentally screaming at the top of my lungs, yet the screams echoed silently in my throat. Finally, my brain touched the surface and the torment ended." Sasha paused to take a deep breath. "I woke up in Purgatory. Jonah and Gabriel were waiting for me and told me I had to get ready to come back to Earth. After a long wait, here I am."

"Amazing," said Ustagov. "You were gone five days down here. How long were you in Purgatory?"

"It felt like months." Sasha shifted her gaze toward Jason. "The only comfort I had was in knowing that, eventually, I'd be back with you."

Jeanette bristled.

"Doctor, you have to remember that time is measured differently in Heaven and Hell." Father Belsario stood up. "A few hours here on Earth correlates to weeks in the other realms. And Purgatory is a no-man's land. None of the rules of Heaven, Hell, or Earth apply." The cleric moved over to the campfire. "If you'll excuse us, Sasha and I have to man our posts for the night watch."

As Sasha stood to join her commander, Jeanette jumped up and stormed off, throwing Jason a hateful glare as she passed. He did not know how to respond.

Haneef took the initiative. "Sook-kyoung and Vicky, check on the horses one final time before turning in. The rest of you, pick up the area and get some sleep."

At first, no one moved. Haneef clapped his hands. "Come

on. Asses and elbows, people."

This time they responded.

As the others left Jason alone, he reached out and petted Lucifer and Lilith, both of whom were curled up beside him. His mind raced with a dozen thoughts at once. He had no problem leading the Demon Hunters across Europe and Asia, battling hordes of Demon Spawn, and closing the portals. When it came to his situation with Jeanette and Sasha, however, he had no idea how to handle it. He loved them both, though in different ways. To be honest, Jason wanted to be with Sasha as much as Jeanette, although that would never happen. That opportunity had long since passed. He still valued her friendship, her advice, and her combat expertise. He needed her as part of the group as someone who provided valuable input and was not be afraid to challenge him if she thought he acted incorrectly. The fact that he often fantasized about Sasha made it more difficult. As for Jeanette, Jason had no idea how to deal with her. Sure, he understood her being angry and jealous that Sasha kept on returning as part of the Purgatoriati. Jason may not be the smartest person in the wasteland, but he was smart enough to know that falling in love with someone while on an expedition as dangerous as this played with fire; a double romance would be disastrous. He wished he could get Jeanette to understand that.

A soft whimper came from his left. Lilith stared at him with her big soulful eyes, sensing his discomfort. He scratched behind her ears.

"You're a good girl."

Lilith's tail wagged furiously.

"I wish I could make Sasha and Jeanette as happy as easily as you."

FATHER BELSARIO WAITED until they were out of earshot

before he spun around and stood in front of Sasha, forcing her to stop short.

"What is wrong with you?"

"I don't understand."

"When you told Jason the only good part about dying was in knowing you would get to come back and be with him again."

"It's the truth," Sasha protested.

"It shouldn't be. I allowed you to come back from Purgatory to help Jason, not to rekindle an old romance."

"I'm not trying to do that." Her words lacked conviction.

"Really? Ever since you met up with us, you've been fawning all over him."

"All right." Sasha walked away, pausing after a few steps. She took a deep breath and faced the cleric. "So maybe I am trying to get Jason to like me again. What's wrong with that?"

"You weren't brought back to Earth to fall in love."

"Why not? Why can't Jason and I be happy? We're probably going to die soon anyway."

"You're already dead." Father Belsario spoke the words like a father who cannot comprehend why his teenager fails to understand his argument. "Not only are you distracting Jason, you're causing problems between him and Jeanette, which is adding to his confusion. He has taken upon himself a difficult enough task and has found a group of people who have enough faith in him to risk their lives for the cause. You're putting them all at risk."

"How?"

"By making Jason think with his heart, not his head. Once he does that, he'll make wrong decisions, decisions that will get people killed, and which will mean the failure of his quest."

Sasha lowered her head, sniffing back the tears. "You don't know how hard it is to keep coming back to life to be with the one you love and not be able to let them know."

Father Belsario's tone softened, though only slightly. "I

admit, I can't relate. But we've been given a chance to accomplish something that is much greater than ourselves."

Sasha did not respond.

Father Belsario sighed with frustration. "If I had my choice, I'd send you back to Purgatory before you do any more damage. I can't. You're here by the grace of God to fulfill a special task."

"Which you won't tell me about."

"Because I can't!" the cleric snapped, and then immediately regretted his outburst. "I'm sorry. I shouldn't have yelled at you."

"It's okay. If I upset you this way, I can only imagine what I'm doing to Jason."

Father Belsario suppressed a grin. Maybe he finally got his point across. "Sasha, you still have free will, so I can't stop you from pursuing Jason if you want. Just remember, if he dies, he's not coming back. It'll be permanent. If you truly love him and are not just doing this for your satisfaction, then leave him alone and let him do what is necessary. Otherwise, what happens from here on is your cross to bear."

The cleric moved past Sasha and went to take up his watch station. Behind him, he heard the young woman sobbing.

CHAPTER TEN

Sook-kyoung and Vicky left to check on the horses. Antoine followed, veering off at the last minute to find a secluded spot in the trees to relieve himself. The two women went from animal to animal, securing each one and making sure they had enough to eat and drink. Sook-kyoung saved her own for last. As she petted its mane and talked to the horse, she heard Vicky crying. Sook-kyoung walked through the pack until she found the young woman leaning against one of the horses, her left arm resting on the animal's side and her face buried against it.

"Is everything all right?"

Vicky stood up and faced her friend. "The horses are fine."

"I was referring to you."

"I'm fine, too."

"Bullshit." Sook-kyoung moved to face Vicky. "What's wrong?"

"I shouldn't be here."

"It's okay to be scared. We all—"

"I'm not scared," Vicky snapped. "Okay, I am. Every single day I struggle to keep it together. But that's not why I shouldn't be here."

"Tell me why."

"I'm a liability to the team." Vicky sniffed back the snot in her nose and used the palms of her hands to wipe away the tears. "Most of you have been fighting Demon Spawn since the portals opened, or you have skills useful to what we're doing. I'm a teenager who worked in my parent's apothecary. The worst I ever dealt with was an angry customer."

"You dealt with a lot worse at Mont St. Michel."

"That was the reason I asked to join Jason's team." Vicky began to cry again. "Because of my selfishness, I've put everyone in danger."

Sook-kyoung hugged Vicky. "We're all in danger, but not because of anything you've done. Jason would never have brought you along if he thought you'd be a liability. As for developing the skills to fight the Demon Spawn, you'll learn those like the rest of us did."

"Are you sure?"

Sook-kyoung broke the hug and stepped back.

"Give it time. Soon you'll be as experienced as the rest of us."

"If she lives that long." Antoine emerged from the trees, zipping up his pants.

"Stop teasing her." Sook-kyoung cut the Moroccan a withering glance that belied the friendliness in her tone.

"I'm telling the truth, which you won't do."

Sook-kyoung turned away. "That's enough."

"No, it's not. She deserves honesty."

"What do you mean?" Vicky asked.

Antoine spoke in a soft manner. "Most of us learned to fight the Demon Spawn by going on search and destroy missions around Mont St. Michel. In the beginning, we only ran into a handful of demons at any one time, which gave us the chance to build up our experience with few losses to the team. All that changed when we started closing the portals. We've lost twenty-two people in France and Russia."

"Casualties are a part of war," Sook-kyoung argued.

"Not at this rate. We've only closed half the known portals at the cost of two-thirds of our people. The odds are not in our favor."

Vicky shook her head in confusion. "Then why did you agree to come?"

"I've done terrible things in my life, things that someone like you can't begin to imagine. The opening of the portals has been a wake-up call that there's an afterlife and that I probably won't fair to well. I've known no other way of life than fighting and violence. I figure if I use those skills to help save the Earth, maybe it'll pay off some of my past sins."

"Do you believe in what we're doing?" Sook-kyoung asked.

"I never said I didn't. What we're doing is noble, and I wouldn't want to be anywhere else." Antoine shifted his attention back to Vicky. "I also want to make sure you understand what you've gotten yourself into. You'll either learn how to battle the Demon Spawn or won't last long enough to let us down. No matter how much experience you get, no matter how skilled in combat you become, the odds are still against you. Only a handful of us will live long enough to be there for the closure of the final portal, if that many. I'm not trying to scare you any more than you already are. I'm just being honest."

Antoine strolled back to camp. Vicky watched him leave.

"He's telling the truth, right?"

Sook-kyoung nodded. "Are you okay?"

"Believe it or not, I feel much better."

"Knowing that your chances of survival are slim?"

"Knowing that I'm not a liability to the team and that I'll pick this up eventually." Vicky feigned a Moroccan accent. "If I last long enough."

Sook-kyoung laughed, and Vicky joined in.

CHAPTER ELEVEN

T HE NEXT MORNING began with the same routine—up early, breakfast, hit the road thirty minutes after sunrise, and travel along miles of highway through uninhabited towns. As had happened over the last five days, the hours dragged by without event.

As the late afternoon sun began its descent toward the horizon, Jason led his team to the crest of a nearby hill to search for a location to spend the night. Through his binoculars, he spotted something unusual. Three miles south long the G1 stood a town like the dozens they had passed since leaving Harbin, except someone had fortified this one. A makeshift wall composed of corrugated iron sheets surrounded the perimeter, supported on the exterior and interior by steel girders welded to the surface and dug into the ground at a forty-five-degree angle. From this distance, Jason guessed the wall to be twenty feet high and well maintained. A closed gate sat on the southbound lanes of the G1. Two enclosed watchtowers stood on either side of the entrance, with similar towers erected along the wall at three-hundred-foot intervals. Jason studied the town for any signs of life, such as movement in the towers or the streets, smoke rising from chimneys, livestock, or tended gardens. After ten minutes, he had not observed anything.

Father Belsario and Ustagov moved their horses beside him. The cleric asked, "What do you see?"

"Not much of anything. Someone fortified that town, but it looks deserted." Jason lowered the binoculars. "Where are we?"

"A sign about a mile back listed it as Shaoguodi." The doctor withdrew his map and studied it for several seconds. "It's so small it's not even listed. The closest town is Biangang-xiang, which is two miles northwest of here."

Haneef, Slava, and Sasha joined them. Sasha maneuvered his horse close to Jason. "What's up?"

Father Belsario motioned toward Shaoguodi. "Someone fortified that town."

Jason raised the binoculars again and scanned the wall. "There's no activity or signs of life. And I'm not detecting any Demon Spawn presence nearby."

"What about human auras?" asked Haneef.

"Nothing."

"Let's go around it," suggested Sasha. "It's small enough that the detour won't take us much out of our way."

"I agree," added Ustagov. "The residents left it for some reason, and I don't want to find out why."

"Maybe they bugged out like everyone else in China," Haneef suggested.

"It's still too risky," warned Ustagov.

"We do need to find a place to bunk down for the night," said Sasha.

"And if the residents bugged out in a hurry," added Slava, "maybe they left behind some supplies."

"If it hasn't already been looted," said Father Belsario.

Jason concentrated on the entrance. "The main gate is closed, and it doesn't look like it's been ransacked."

Ustagov rubbed his eyes in frustration. "Why don't you go up, knock on the door, and see if anyone's home?"

Jason slid the binoculars back in their case. "That's a good idea."

"I was being sarcastic."

"I know. It's still the best option." Jason scanned the surrounding area for several seconds before pointing to a small hillock south of the G1 eight hundred feet from the compound. "Haneef, take the team over there and wait on the leeward side. If anything happens, cover us. Father Belsario and Slava, you're with me."

Jason gave his team time to cross the field to the hillock. At first, Lucifer and Lilith stayed beside him, refusing to leave. Only after Sasha called the werehounds did they reluctantly trot off to be with her. Once the others had taken up position, Jason, Father Belsario, and Slava urged their horses forward. The three men took as non-menacing an appearance as possible, with Jason and Slava keeping their AK-47s slung over their shoulders; Jason unbuttoned his winter coat and pulled the flaps aside to show he did not conceal any weapons. He shifted his eyes from one tower to the next, searching for movement, and checked the road ahead for traps or tripwires. They approached within three hundred feet of the wall and still no signs of activity. With luck, the gate would be unlocked, and there would still be something useful inside for them to stock up on.

A loud buzz passed Jason's left ear. He leaned to the right and waved his hand across the left side of his face, hoping to shoo away the insect. A second buzzed by. Jason thought they had disturbed a nest. Then he heard the distinctive sound of a bullet ricocheting off metal and, out of the corner of his eye, saw a spark fly off Father Belsario's breastplate. It took a moment for the reality to settle in.

"Someone's shooting at us!" The cleric spun his horse around.

Jason focused his attention back on the wall. A flash of gunfire emanated from a slit in the side of one of the watchtowers. A bullet passed by his head and thudded into flesh. Father Belsario groaned and clutched his back near the abdomen. A circle of blood stained the cleric's cloak and seeped between his fingers.

Damn it, Jason chastised himself. *The residents suckered them into an ambush.*

Jason spurred his horse and yelled, "Head for cover!"

HANEEF HEARD THE first two shots yet had no idea where they came from. He scanned the wall and saw the third round being fired.

"Father Belsario's been hit," Jonah cried out.

Jason and the others were caught in the open. Haneef knew he had to get them out of there or they would be cut to pieces. He raised his AK-47.

"I want suppressing fire on those watchtowers. Now!"

RETURN FIRE ERUPTED from the hillock, pelting the firing positions on each tower and silencing the incoming rounds from the town. Jason took advantage of the temporary lull and raced for cover, while Slava stayed close by him with Father Belsario slightly behind, hunched over in his saddle. They had ridden a hundred feet when Haneef and the others expended their ammunition and paused to reload, which allowed the attackers to emerge from behind cover and resume fire.

Slava's horse whinnied as a bullet tore into its right rear thigh. The animal toppled to the side, throwing Slava. He wrapped his arms around his head and lowered his chin into his chest so he wouldn't break his neck in the fall. The Russian landed on his back and, for a moment, blacked out. Although dazed and winded, he had the presence of mind to seek safety. He crawled toward his wounded horse, collapsing face-first into the dirt. Slava hid behind the animal as two more rounds slammed into it. One bullet punched through its abdomen, missing Slava by inches and splattering him with blood. The horse yelped and kicked violently for a moment before going limp.

"Get to safety," Jason ordered Father Belsario. "I'm going

to rescue Slava."

Jason spun his horse around and galloped back for his friend.

"SHIT!" HANEEF WATCHED Slava topple from his horse, although he could not tell if he had been shot or thrown off. He felt sick when Jason headed into the gunfire to save him.

"Use single shots. Keep their heads down for as long as possible."

Sasha sidled up beside him. "It won't be enough. We have to draw away fire."

"How are we going to do that?"

As she thought, Jonah and Gabriel rushed out from cover to rescue Father Belsario, the former grabbing the horse's reins and leading it to safety while the latter propped up the cleric in his saddle. Rounds from the towers kicked up dirt around them.

"I have an idea."

Calling for Matthew and Luther to join her, Sasha explained her plan. The three Purgatoriati mounted their horses. Sasha rode around the right flank of the hillock and the other two headed for the left. Once clear of cover, the trio veered their horses toward the town, zigzagging as they stormed the gate from two different directions. As expected, the shooters switched their attention from Jason and Slava to those charging the wall. Leaning forward, she covered the left side of the horse's neck and head as best she could with her body.

Sasha hoped this worked. She may have been immortal, but she was not immune from pain.

JASON RODE UP behind Slava. He did not have much time.

"Get on!"

Slava climbed to his feet, his left arm dangling beside him.

Reaching out and taking his right hand, Jason helped the Russian climb onto the back of his horse. A bullet whizzed by the animal's head, causing it to buck. Slava slid back to the ground.

"Get out of here," he ordered. "I can make it on foot."

"You won't make it very far."

The gunfire shifted away from him and Slava as Sasha, Matthew, and Luther drew attention away from them. They had only a few seconds. Jason held out his hand. "Move your ass."

Slava grabbed the hand and hoisted himself up, this time sliding behind Jason. Spinning his horse in the direction of the hillock, Jason rode as fast as possible for cover.

SASHA ATTEMPTED TO create as much of a distraction as possible. She charged the front gate, weaving in no pattern so the attackers could not predict her next move, hoping to draw enough fire onto her so Jason and Slava could get away. It worked. An increasing number of rounds slammed into the dirt around her or passed close by, one tearing through the folds of her cloak. Off to her left, Matthew and Luther were drawing away the rest of the fire. Thank God the attackers were firing single shots; if this had been automatic weapon's fire, none of them would have made it this far.

When Jason and Slava reached the hillock, Sasha broke off her diversionary charge and headed back. At that moment, the gunfire from the town shifted onto Jason again. Her heart sank when his body jerked and a cloud of blood formed around his shoulder.

JASON HAD MADE it to within a few yards of the safety of the hillock when the barrage of bullets shifted in his direction. Two passed by his head close enough that he could hear them, the rest punched harmlessly into the ground. In a couple of seconds, he and Slava would—

A bolt of pain shot through him as a bullet slammed into his left shoulder. The force of the blow pushed him forward and would have knocked him out of his saddle if Slava hadn't grabbed his waist and held him in place. An agony he had never experienced before replaced the initial shock. Thankfully, his horse rounded the hillock before any other rounds found their mark.

Lilith and Lucifer rushed over to greet him, the latter standing on his hind legs and resting his front paws on the horse's flank to get closer to his master. Jason leaned over to pet him. As he did, another jolt of pain shot down his arm, momentarily clogging his thinking. Jeanette and Ustagov joined him a moment later.

"Oh my God," Jeanette gasped as she saw the blood staining his winter coat.

Ustagov moved her out of the way to examine the wound. "I can't tell from here. It doesn't look fatal, though. You're not gushing blood, so the bullet didn't hit an artery. Come down and let me check it."

"Later. Right now, we have to get out of here." Jason shook his head to clear his mind. "Fall back and regroup."

Sasha rode up a moment later, moving up on Jason's right. When she got her first good luck at the wound, her eyes widened in fear. "Will you be okay?"

"I'll be fine," Jason replied.

"Are you sure?"

"No, he's not," Ustagov protested. "And I won't know for certain until he allows me to examine him."

"It can wait." Jason's tone warned there would be no further discussion. At that moment, Matthew and Luther rode around the other side of the hillock. "Everybody mount up and follow me. And keep your eyes open in case they try to follow us."

A minute later, Jason led his team north up the G1.

CHAPTER TWELVE

J ASON TOOK HIS team two miles up the G1 until they were out of sight of Shaoguodi. They then headed west, circling around Biangangxiang and making their way through fallow farmland and fields. He avoided every town and village in case lookouts had been placed there. To be certain they were not being followed, he asked Luther and Gabriel to fall back and watch their rear. Two hours after sunset, the team came upon a wooded area located eight miles southwest of Shaoguodi and isolated from other population centers. Jason ordered everyone to settle down for the night and to keep the horses tied up nearby in case they needed to make a quick escape. As the others tended to their preparations and organized the watch, Gaston built a fire and made a deflector shield out of tree branches and blankets to prevent the flames from being observed by any search parties that might be scouting for them. Twenty minutes after camp had been set up, Jason, Slava, and Father Belsario sat around the fire having their wounds tended to by Ustagov and Vicky. Lucifer and Lilith stayed close by Jason, who had his flight suit unzipped and pulled down around his waist. He draped the blood-stained winter coat over his right shoulder and side to keep warm. Jeanette and Sasha sat beside the werehounds, petting them.

Ustagov opened a bottle of rubbing alcohol, wet a clean cloth, and dabbed the open wound. Jason gasped.

"Damn, that hurts."

"It's going to hurt a lot more as it heals."

Jason remained stoic. "How bad is it?"

"You lucked out."

"Are you serious? I was shot."

"It's a clean wound. It went through muscle and did little damage." Ustagov reached into his medic's bag and withdrew the sewing kit. "An inch to the left and the bullet would have punctured your artery and you would have bled out. An inch to the right and it would have shattered your shoulder blade. The downside is I can't properly fix it out here in the field, so you may lose some mobility in your arm."

"It's better than the alternative."

"That's for sure." Ustagov turned to Vicky. "How's Slava's arm?"

"It's not broken, and I don't think it's fractured."

"Are you sure?" Slava asked. "It's killing me."

Ustagov stepped over and felt the limb. Slava winced.

"What's the pain level on a scale of one to ten?"

"Five." Slave shrugged. "Maybe six."

"If you had broken your arm you'd be experiencing a steady ten." The doctor placed one hand under Slava's forearm and raised it at a ninety-degree angle.

"Shit!"

"You bruised the muscles pretty bad when you fell. You're going to be in a lot of pain for the next week or two, but it'll heal. Exercise it and keep it active so the muscles don't get stiff. Vicky will give you some pain meds."

"Morphine?" Slava asked hopefully.

"Ibuprofen."

"Thanks," said Slava with much less enthusiasm.

Ustagov patted Slava on his good shoulder. After Vicky handed the Russian four caplets, the doctor asked her, "Do you know how to stitch a wound?"

"I once watched my dad sew up a neighbor's arm."

"Finish off Jason, please. I want to check on Father Belsario."

"No need for that," said the cleric, who sat propped up

against a tree. "I'll be fine."

"I doubt that. You took a bullet to the gut. It'll be a miracle if it doesn't go septic."

"The wound will heal on its own in a day or two."

"You're in pain, right?"

The cleric nodded.

Ustagov reached into the medic's bag. "Let me give you something to ease it."

"Save it for someone else. It won't work on me."

"Are you sure?"

"We don't need food, water, or sleep because they do not affect us. The same holds true for medicine."

"Let me know if you change your mind."

Father Belsario nodded and laid back against the tree to rest.

"I'd like to know why that town fired on us without warning," said Jeanette. "We weren't a threat."

"They were probably paranoid." Jason winced as Vicky inserted the needle underneath the skin on his shoulder. Lucifer whimpered and tried to go over to him; Sasha held him and scratched behind his ears.

"No one would blame them after what this world has become." Ustagov sat down in front of the fire and took a drink from his canteen. "We can't rule out the possibility that there's a serious threat somewhere out here."

"What do you mean?" asked Jeanette.

Ustagov screwed the top back on the canteen. "That town was the first people we've seen since arriving at Harbin. Everyone else cleared out a long time ago."

"Maybe they're dead," offered Sasha.

"We'd have come across the bodies. This part of China isn't devastated, it's abandoned. Maybe there's a horde of Demon Spawn roaming the countryside we haven't run into yet, though I doubt it. If that were the case, you'd think that town would be happy to have others join their ranks, as we did with you in Moscow. My guess is there's a group of humans out here so scary the locals will shoot anyone who comes near."

"What he says makes sense," said Slava.

"That also puts us in an unenviable position," added Father Belsario. "If the doctor is correct, that means not only can't we trust anyone we come across, they might also prove as big a threat to us as the demons."

"Shit." This time Jason directed his cussing toward the situation and not the pain in his shoulder.

"So how do we proceed?" Jeanette asked.

"No change in plans, just a change in tactics. I want to stay off the road for the next few days in case the residents of that town decide to hunt us. Doc, plot a route to Shenyang that avoids areas of population."

"It won't be easy. The closer we get to the city, the more towns and villages we'll run into."

"I understand but do your best. The longer we can delay another run-in with the locals the better our chances of figuring out how to survive them. Slava, do you feel well enough to make the rounds and brief those on watch about what we discussed."

"I do."

"The rest of you get some sleep. We have to replace those on watch in a few hours."

Slava went off to update the rest of the team and Ustagov went back to the horses to retrieve the map. A few minutes later, Vicky finished stitching the wound and covered it with a bandage. "Done."

"Thanks."

"Do you need any painkillers?"

Jason rolled his shoulder. The pain was excruciating, yet he refused to admit it. "I'll be fine."

"Let me know if you change your mind." She squeezed his good shoulder. "Your fan club is waiting."

As Vicky left, Lucifer jumped up and trotted over to Jason.

The werehound sniffed the wound for several seconds and licked around the bandage. Jason wrapped his good arm around Lucifer's neck, pulled him close, and kissed him on the top of his head. Lilith rushed over to get in on the affection. When he finally got a chance to breathe, Jason nodded to Sasha.

"Thanks for saving our lives today."

Sasha beamed. "You're welcome."

"That was quick thinking on your part." Jason slid on the upper portion of his flight suit, grimacing as he maneuvered his left arm into the sleeve. "Slava and I might not be here if it wasn't for you."

"I was worried about you." Sasha realized her comment came out wrong and backtracked. "I mean all three of you."

Jeanette stood and stormed off.

Sasha sighed and her shoulders slumped. "Sorry. I don't mean to cause problems between you two."

"It's not your fault."

"Yes, it is." Sasha got to her feet, all the time avoiding eye contact. "I have to go keep watch. I'll check on you in the morning."

Lucifer watched Sasha leave and glanced up at his master with a confused expression on his face. Jason shrugged, not entirely sure he knew what had happened. He did not notice the stern, disapproving glower Father Belsario gave Sasha as she departed.

When she stepped out of earshot, Jason scooted closer to Father Belsario. "Can I ask you a question?"

"Sure."

"How come none of the others who have died, like Werner and Neal, have come back as Purgatoriati?"

"Only those consigned to Purgatory can return to Earth. My guess is that your team members who died in combat have all ascended into Heaven."

"Or gone to Hell?"

Father Belsario chuckled. "Considering all that you've done, and the sacrifices you've made to rid the world of the portals, I'm confident their previous sins have been forgiven, and they've been granted salvation."

"I hope you're right." Jason thought for a moment. "I have another question."

"Go ahead."

"You intimated earlier that Sasha has a pivotal role to play in the closing of the portals. What type of role?"

The cleric grew somber. "I can't tell you."

"Can't or won't?"

"Both." Father Belsario held up a hand, cutting off Jason. "There is no mythical prophecy that Sasha is fulfilling that I'm hiding from you. However, there are certain aspects of being a member of the Purgatoriati, when combined with Sasha's affection for you, which could prove decisive in the future."

"And you won't tell me anything more?"

"If I did, it could negatively influence what you need to do."

"You're saying that if I know what you do, it might cause me to make decisions that would result in us not closing the portals?"

"Nothing that severe."

"At least you're not vague," Jason said sarcastically.

"Sorry."

Jason paused for several moments as he absorbed the information. "One more question. Will how I treat Sasha have an impact on whether we succeed?"

Father Belsario shook his head. "No."

"Good."

"Can I offer a friendly word of advice? I realize you and Sasha have strong feelings for each other and may want to consummate them. I understand that, but caution against it. What you two do together will have little impact on how events play out." Father Belsario stood, taking a moment to steady his

73

legs. "However, how you feel about Sasha, especially when you find out what is special about her, could have a major impact on a personal decision you may face. That's a call you alone will have to make, and something only you will have to live with. Choose wisely."

The cleric limped away, leaving Jason alone with the were-hounds.

QIANG WATCHED THE outsiders from half a mile away from an old irrigation ditch that cut through the farmland adjacent to the woods. Those near the campfire were relatively easy to make out, while the others blended into the shadows. He assessed the latter posed no threat to him unless he attempted to approach, which he had no intention of doing. At this stage, he only wanted to observe their behavior and determine their motivations, yet that raised as many questions as it answered, and piqued his fascination with the outsiders.

"They don't act like the others," Min whispered, even though he stood only two feet from Qiang. "They withdrew from Shaoguodi rather than attack."

"That doesn't mean they don't pose a threat. You saw the way they extradited themselves from that situation. These people are militarily trained, which means they could cause trouble."

"What do you want to do about them?"

Qiang thought for a moment. He had ruled out the possibility that the outsiders were simply passing through; they seemed determined to reach Shenyang as soon as possible, which meant they would be in his territory for quite a while. That left only one viable option.

"Have Deng go back and round up the others. Once we have the numbers, we'll contact these people and find out if they're friendly or if they need to be eliminated."

CHAPTER THIRTEEN

THE NEXT MORNING, only Father Belsario felt better, the pain having subsided from excruciating to piercing. Slava could barely move his left arm when he woke because the muscles ached so badly. Jason's wound throbbed from the front of his shoulder all the way to the back, and it only grew worse after being jostled around in a saddle.

The team made their way toward Shenyang through the open territory west of the G1, detouring around any towns or villages they came across, thankfully without incident. They had traveled all morning, took a lunch break near an old grain silo, and continued. Shortly after noon, a steady breeze rose from the south. Twenty minutes later, a strong gust wafted over them, bringing with it a stench both sickeningly sweet and nauseatingly disgusting.

"What smells so bad?" Antoine asked.

Jeanette gagged. "It's horrible."

"It reminds me of the slaughterhouse outside the town where I grew up," said Slava.

"Except the slaughterhouses all shut down with the EMP." Jason steered his horse toward Ustagov, who had already removed his map and laid it out in his saddle. "Do you have any idea where we are?"

The doctor studied the map. "According to this, we're thirty-five miles north of Changchun in the middle of nowhere. The closest village is five miles away."

Another gust blew from the south, again bringing with it the horrible stench. Gaston leaned to one side and vomited.

Lilith and Lucifer huddled closer to Jason's horse.

"What is that?" Ian asked.

"There's only one way to find out," answered Jason. He pointed to a rise a mile away. "It's coming from that direction."

"That may not be a good idea," warned Father Belsario.

"I agree," added Haneef. "We have no idea what's causing that."

"We're going to find out one way or the other." Jason spurred his horse in that direction. "I'd rather do it on my terms."

The others fell in behind him and unslung their AK-47s, laying them across their laps. The Purgatoriati pushed their cloaks aside for easy access to their swords. Jason cleared his mind and allowed his senses to scan the area. He did not detect any auras of Demon Spawn. In fact, he sensed nothingness, an absence in the realm, although he could not quite put his finger on it. However, he could not entirely rely on his sixth sense because it could only detect demons with souls, and not the insects they encountered in the Paris underground or the dragons in Red Square. God only knew what awaited them when they topped the rise. For a moment, Jason considered falling back and avoiding the area. He shook off that idea. Whatever they found might offer a clue to the location of the portal.

The group reached the base of the rise and ascended. A loud buzzing came from the other side. All those who had been attacked by the giant wasps outside of Falaise raised their weapons into the high-ready position. Jason almost ordered them to stand down. As his horse crested the hill, he braced himself for what they would find.

Nothing could have prepared Jason for the sight before him.

Scores of human corpses lay strewn across a grassy field, or, more precisely, what remained of the bodies. The skeletons had been picked clean of flesh and organs, leaving only cartilage and gristle attached to bones. Tattered clothes, strips of flesh, and chunks of body parts littered the ground. Dried blood stained the grass dark brown. The buzzing came from thousands of flies and wasps that covered the carnage and fed off the remains.

"Dear God," Vicky whispered.

Father Belsario closed his eyes and crossed himself.

"Who could have done this?" Antoine asked.

"It had to be ravagers," answered Gaston. "Nothing else could cause such damage."

"It's not ravagers," said Ustagov.

"How do you know?"

"Ravagers would have ripped these people apart, not picked their bones clean."

"Maybe they were attacked and eaten by wild animals?" offered Sasha.

"Wild animals would have eaten the other body parts as well." Ustagov nudged his horse down the rise.

"Where are you going?" Jason asked.

"I want to get a closer look at the bodies."

"It's too dangerous."

"It may be more dangerous not to," said the doctor.

"Damn." Jason shifted his horse sideways. "Sasha and Sook-kyoung are with me. The rest of you stay here and watch for any signs of danger."

"I should go," offered Father Belsario.

"You're still healing. Stay here. We'll be back in a minute."

By the time they reached the bottom of the rise, Ustagov had dismounted. He removed a medical face mask from his jacket and wrapped it around his mouth and nose, and then cautiously waded into the decimation field so as not to disturb the insects. Jason and Sasha dismounted a hundred feet from the edge of the carnage, gave Sook-kyoung the reins to their horses, and followed the doctor. Every step disturbed a swarm of flies and wasps that hovered around their faces. The insects were such a nuisance they overwhelmed the stomach-churning stench. Jason covered his mouth and nose with his hand and occasionally shook his head to dislodge them. They caught up with Ustagov as he knelt beside a small skeleton.

"These are the remains of a child about five years old." Ustagov ran his hand along the bones, kicking up a black cloud of flies.

"What are you looking for?" Jason asked.

"I'll know if I find it. Give me a few minutes."

Jason noticed something in the grass a few feet away and walked over to it. He bent down, brushed away the insects, and picked it up. It was a stuffed panda. Blood stained the underside that had lain against the grass. It had lost one of its eyes, and a tiny crimson handprint stained one of its paws. He dropped the toy back onto the grass, disturbing a swarm that buzzed angrily around him. A wasp stung him in the leg.

Ustagov moved from one skeleton to the next, examining the remains attached to the bones. At one point, he stopped by an insect-covered mound, carefully brushed them away, and picked up a slice of human skin three feet long. Rummaging through the pile, he lifted two more pieces of skin the same length and cut. Continuing his search, the doctor stopped several more times, pushing around something with the toe of his boot before examining it.

"Are you almost ready?" Jason spat a fly out of his mouth.

"In a minute."

"Hurry up. I'm getting eaten alive out here."

"Trust me. You don't want to rush me on this."

Not able to take the insects any longer, Jason moved to the edge of the decimation field. Sasha accompanied him. Jason shook his head and ran his fingers through his hair, dislodging several flies. A few minutes later, Ustagov joined them. He held a strip of human flesh in his hand.

"What's that?" Jason asked.

"It's bad news." Ustagov removed his face mask.

"Do you know what ate them?" Sasha asked.

"Those bodies weren't eaten."

"Then what happened to the flesh and internal organs?"

Ustagov handed the strip of flesh to Sasha, who examined it and passed it to Jason. The edges appeared as if they had been cut with a scalpel. "These pieces of flesh, like the bits of organs I found out there, were sliced away rather than chewed or torn off."

"You mean their flesh and organs were surgically removed?" Jason asked.

"Yes, in a very crude manner."

Jason scanned the decimation field. "So where did it all go? Did they take it away to eat later?"

Ustagov took a deep breath. "Do you remember back in Moscow when I showed you the Golem I had dissected?"

"Yes. Each organ and limb was made of several hundred human body parts…. Wait a minute. Are you suggesting…?"

Ustagov nodded. "These people were stripped clean and their parts used to create a new Golem."

"How?"

"I don't know the process." The doctor raised his hand holding the strip of flesh. "This is exactly like the strips of flesh I found on the Golem from Moscow."

"Where is it now?" Sasha scanned the area.

"Maybe guarding the portal or maybe off hunting for us. I don't know." Ustagov tossed the strip of flesh back onto the field. It barely hit the ground when a swarm of flies covered it. "This confirms one thing."

"What's that?" Jason asked.

"We're near the portal."

CHAPTER FOURTEEN

LEAVING THE DECIMATION field behind them, Jason led the team south until dusk. The tension was palpable. In one sense, finding the field had been reassuring since it confirmed they were traveling in the right direction. However, the sight had unnerved them. They had all witnessed their fair share of bloodshed and carnage, although none had ever seen something so disturbing. Jason guessed there probably were more sites like this scattered around northern China. He hoped they did not run across them.

That night they settled down in a rusted warehouse that had not been used for years. Cobwebs and dust covered the interior, and it took over an hour to clean the area enough to be comfortable. Jason knew the busy work would keep his team's mind off the decimation field. Dinner was quiet and sullen, with a lot of forced small talk. After everyone had eaten, and the first watch had joined the Purgatoriati on guard duty, Jason waited nearly an hour. He then left the werehounds with Sook-kyoung and made his way toward Jeanette's watch post.

When Jeanette heard him approaching, she spun around, at first thinking he might be a demon. Her initial expression of surprise changed to one of concern. "Is everything okay?"

"Everything's fine. We need to talk."

Jeanette became cold and angry and turned away. "There's nothing to talk about."

"Yes, there is."

"Well, I'm on duty."

"We need to talk right now." Jason moved in front of Jeanette. "You've been ignoring me for days."

"That's because you've been busy with your precious Sasha."

"Knock it off. I need everyone concentrating on the task at hand and not acting like this is high school."

The forcefulness of Jason's outburst startled Jeanette. For a moment she stared at him, shocked that he spoke to her in that tone. Then she bristled. "Roger that, sir."

Jason sighed, regretting how he had snapped. "Don't be like that."

"How do you want me to be?"

"I understand you're jealous about Sasha. You have no reason to be."

"Really? She's been flirting with you ever since she came back from the dead, and you love every minute of it."

"Sasha and I have known each other since the beginning of the apocalypse. She's only a friend."

Jeanette frowned and walked away, mumbling something under her breath.

"What was that?"

"I said, 'sometimes I think we're just friends.'"

"That's not fair. I wanted us to be closer. You kept telling me you weren't ready."

"I'm ready now." Jeanette spun around to face him. "I told you a week ago I wanted to make love to you before something happens to one of us, and you changed the subject. How can I not think you don't really care?"

"You don't understand." Jason wasn't sure he understood his own emotions. "I've had to reevaluate my priorities. I've already lost too many people I've cared for."

"Like Sasha." Jeanette spat the words.

"And my mother and Doc. If I make love to you and then lose you, I don't know if I'd be able to carry on."

"How will you feel if you never make love to me and I get killed? Will you regret it? Or will you shrug your shoulders and move on to…?" Jeanette inhaled, holding her breath for ten seconds before exhaling slowly. "I know you have strong feelings for me, but I don't think you really love me."

"That's not it."

"Then what is it?" Jeanette pleaded.

Jason knew why he hesitated to consummate their relationship, and it had nothing to do with his lack of feelings toward Jeanette. He had wanted to be intimate with her since they arrived at Mont St. Michel. That changed after a hundred ravagers attacked the armored train near Lake Baikal and the nightmarish battle that ensued. It brought back memories of how he used to obsess about Sasha, and how he had become distracted during crisis situations worrying about her. That was before he became the team's leader. He could no longer afford such an emotional luxury. The task they undertook was too important, and too many people relied on Jason for him to be constantly checking on Jeanette. How could he tell the woman he loved that she took second place to everyone else in the world?

Jeanette huffed. "If you can't answer me, then this conversation is—"

The noise originated in the west and rapidly drew closer. It sounded like a freight train. Jason and Jeanette unslung their AK-47s and aimed into the dark, not knowing what monstrosity would emerge from the shadows. The nearby trees swayed for a moment, and the field bulged and rolled toward them in a wave. As it passed by, the ground jerked, like being in a moving vehicle that hit a speed bump, before continuing toward the warehouse. The walls shook and windows rattled, and from inside the structure came shouting and the frightened whinnying of horses. Lilith and Lucifer rushed outside and made their way to Jason, wanting to make certain of his safety. By the time those who had been in the warehouse emerged, the wave had moved on.

"What was that?" Vicky asked.

"Are we under attack?" Antoine chimed in.

"Calm down, mates." Ian raised his hands to get everyone's attention. "It was only a bloody earth tremor."

"You mean an earthquake?" Slava asked.

"A small one. We get them all the time along the Pacific Rim."

A sense of relief washed over the group.

Jason clapped his hands to get their attention. "Okay, back to guard duty or back to bed. We have a long night ahead of us."

Half his team returned to the warehouse, although Jason knew it would take a while for those who were not on duty to fall asleep. Lucifer and Lilith stayed with him. When Jason went to finish his conversation, Jeanette had moved away and taken up her guard position several hundred feet from him. He knew enough to take the hint. Reaching down and scratching his pets behind the ears, Jason led the werehounds to the warehouse.

CHAPTER FIFTEEN

T HE NEXT TWO days passed without incident, other than experiencing several more earth tremors. Jason had decided to avoid Changchun and circle around it to the west, again maneuvering the team between towns and villages to avoid hostile human contact. On the third day, they swung south, hoping to link back up to the G1. After lunch, as the others cleaned the area and prepared to move out, Jason and Ustagov consulted the map.

"Where are we now?"

Ustagov ran his finger across its surface and stopped. "We're right here, approximately five miles from the G1 halfway between Changchun and Siping. It should be another week to Shenyang."

"If the portal is near Shenyang."

"Don't be so pessimistic." Ustagov folded the map and slipped it under his jacket. "Finding that field of the dead proves we're heading in the r—"

"Excuse me." Slava walked up and pointed with his good arm to the west. Jason and Ustagov looked in that direction. Two miles away, a tan-colored cloud rolled across the ground, spreading north and south as far as they could see. Several buildings in the distance, including a large one made of cement, disappeared as the cloud engulfed them.

"Do either of you have any idea what that is?" the Russian asked.

"It's a dust storm," said Ustagov.

"Are you sure it's not a cover for something demonic, like

in that Stephen King movie?"

"I'm sure."

"I didn't think we were near any deserts," said Jason.

"We're not." Ustagov headed back to his horse. "It probably came from Mongolia or western China."

Jason followed. "Is it dangerous?"

"If we get caught in it, it could be." By now the doctor had reached the others, who bombarded him with questions. He raised his hands to silence them. "We're going to be fine. The biggest danger is from suffocation. We have the gas masks Svetlana gave us, and we can wrap wet cloths around the horses' noses. The storm is moving slowly. If we head southeast as fast as we can, we should be able to find a place to shelter before it reaches us."

"Sounds like a plan to me," said Haneef.

"Get out your masks and prep the horses," ordered Jason. "We move out in three minutes."

The team had readied their horses, and half had climbed into their saddles, when they heard the familiar rumbling of an approaching earth tremor. Jason maneuvered his horse to face west. The bulging ground emerged from out of the dust storm and rushed towards them. He warned everyone to be ready for the bump as it rolled past and his team braced themselves. However, the wave never swept by. It slowed, stopping two hundred feet away. A moment later, the ground swelled, rising five feet. The bulge collapsed, leaving a crater twenty feet in circumference and ten feet deep. The area around it undulated and the rumbling increased, this time louder and faster. Before Jason had a chance to order his team to run, the crater burst open, showering them with earth and gravel.

A giant worm rose from the center, eight feet in diameter and towering thirty feet above them. The segmented body glistened blood red underneath the coating of dirt. The setae along its length bristled. Its thorax bent toward the ground. A giant mouth, seven feet in width, dominated the head. Four rows of fangs descended into it, each row two feet apart from the other, with fangs ranging in size from eighteen inches in front to six in back. Its prostomium, the tongue-like lobe that the worm used to sense its surroundings, extended. It stretched for twenty-five feet and swished through the air. After several seconds, the prostomium retracted.

Without warning, the thorax plunged to the ground toward Father Belsario. He fell to his right, dropping out of his saddle at the last moment. Instead, the worm's mouth engulfed his horse. The animal thrashed about in terror and whinnied in agony as the first row of fangs sunk through its skin and into its muscles, clasping it tightly. The first row retracted, pulling the horse into the worm's mouth where the second row surged forward, dug into the terrified animal, and drew it farther in. The horse thrashed about, trying to break free, causing more damage to itself. All four sets of fangs worked in tandem, biting and retracting until the horse had been dragged into the demon's esophagus.

"Run!"

Jason yelled the command, although the warning was unnecessary. Everyone had already swung their horses around and galloped at full speed to the southeast. Gabriel paused long enough to help Father Belsario into the saddle behind him before racing off after the others. The worm's prostomium detected the movement from Gabriel's horse, and the head lunged, the fangs slamming into the dirt two feet behind the animal. Jason glanced back as the thorax disappeared back into the crater.

"*Merde!*"

The cry came from Antoine. A second worm had broken through the ground in front of the team. Sook-kyoung could not stop in time. Her horse ran into the demon, toppling over and throwing her from the saddle. She hit the ground with a heavy gasp, rolled twice, and lay motionless. The worm bent over and clutched the horse around its head, the four rows of fangs beginning the agonizing process of devouring its prey.

Gaston spurred his horse forward and maneuvered around the worm, racing toward Sook-kyoung. He stopped, dismounted, and ran toward her. "Can you hear me? Are you—"

A third worm broke through the ground directly under Gaston's feet. He dropped into its mouth up to his abdomen before the first row of fangs closed around his waist. A gut-wrenching scream escaped from his lips. Despite the crippling wounds, he tried to climb out. Gaston's fingers frantically dug at the worm's slimy flanks, unable to get a firm grip. It would not have made a difference. The undulation of the fangs pulled him deeper inside. They sliced through his skin and punctured his organs, as though dozens of daggers plunged into his body at once, rupturing his stomach and shredding his intestines. By now he should have passed out from agony and loss of blood; fear and the desperate desire to survive kept him conscious. He panicked when he felt his feet dangling at the tip of the creature's esophagus, knowing what would happen next. Gaston struggled to break free, but with decreasing vigor. The worm belched, and he smelled the gaseous stench of its stomach wafting up, which caused him to puke. He gagged on his own blood and vomitus. His clouded eyes pleaded for help he knew would never come. Finally, the first row of fangs closed around Gaston's head and dragged him to his gastronomic death.

Gaston's horse bolted and headed toward the G1, galloping at full tilt. It had traveled fifty feet when the first worm burst through the ground to its right. As the horse raced past, its thorax bent, and its mouth latched onto the animal's back. The horse bucked and kicked. Because of the angle in which the worm had bitten, it could not pull the animal into its mouth, so it released its grip. The horse fell to the ground with a thud. It flayed around in the dirt, too severely wounded to get up. Lowering itself to the ground, the worm slithered across the field, circling its prey to come in from behind. The other two worms disappeared into their craters, the one feasting on Sook-kyoung's horse spitting out the animal's remains as it disappeared. They reemerged on the opposite side of Gaston's horse. The three creatures ripped the animal to shreds as each attempted to feed.

"Shit," said Ustagov.

"What is it?" Jason asked.

"Those things detect sound waves on the surface. That's how they homed in on Sook-kyoung and Gaston."

"If we stay still, they know we're here and will keep searching until they find us."

Ustagov thought for a moment. "We have a chance if we head into the storm. The noise of the dust scraping across the surface might mask our movements. Even if it doesn't, once above ground their sensory receptors will be useless."

"That storm is a mile and a half away. How do we get to it before those worms get to us?"

"I have an idea."

Jason spun his horse around. "I hope you know what you're doing."

"So do I."

"No time to explain," Jason yelled to the others. "We're heading into the dust storm. Do exactly what the doctor tells you and we might make it out of this alive."

"What about the anti-matter device?" Haneef asked. "Sook-kyoung carried one of them."

"We'll come back for it."

Nudging his horse in the abdomen, Jason headed toward the storm with the others trailing after him. Lilith and Lucifer stayed close by their master. Soon the team rode at full speed.

Detecting the vibrations, the three worms descended back into the ground and set off in pursuit.

CHAPTER SIXTEEN

A S JASON'S TEAM raced toward the dust storm, Ustagov kept checking over his shoulder. The first time, the worms were still visible, feeding on Gaston's horse. The next time, they had disappeared, and three waves headed straight for them. He timed it carefully, calculating the speed of the horses with that of the worms. When the waves vanished, Ustagov knew the creatures were diving before resurfacing.

"On me!"

The doctor veered his horse right and the others followed. A moment later, the three worms broke through the earth where Jason's team would have been if they had kept going straight. After a few seconds, the worms descended beneath the surface and the triple waves rushed toward them. Ustagov waited for the worms to dive before swerving left. Again, the creatures broke through where Jason's team should have been. By now, several of the others had figured out the doctor's intentions and kept their own eyes on the worms' progress, maneuvering out of the way before they resurfaced. They kept this up for several minutes, avoiding the creatures and closing the gap with the approaching dust storm.

Through everyone performing their own maneuvers, the team had broken up into smaller groups that were now spread out. Jeanette, Antoine, Ian, and Vicky were more than half a mile to the left. Even more troubling, the waves were no longer visible. Jason sidled his horse up near Ustagov.

"The worms aren't following us. Do you think they gave up?"

The doctor checked over his shoulder and muttered a single word. "Shit."

"What's wrong?"

"They didn't give up. They're learning."

The worms broke through the surface in a triangular formation directly in front of Jason's team.

SOOK-KYOUNG GROANED AS she tried to push herself up. The muscles in her chest and arms ached. Her vision blurred, so she closed her eyes for a moment to clear it. She barely remembered what happened. She recalled heading south away from the giant worm—

She rolled onto her back, half expecting a fanged head to be hovering over her, ready to consume its meal. The only thing nearby was the partially-devoured carcass of her horse. Crawling to her feet, she wondered where the rest of the team had gone. Then she recalled the second worm bursting through beside her and tossing her into the air like a ragdoll. She searched for the rest of the team but could not find them. Had they left her because they thought she was dead? Were they forced to escape certain death? Or was she the only one still alive?

Gunfire to the west attracted Sook-kyoung's attention. Over a mile away, the rest of the team battled the worms. She considered joining them and ruled out the possibility. Even if she could make it that far without one of the creatures hunting her down, the dust storm would engulf the team well before she reached them. Her best chance lay in heading southeast and finding shelter. Once the storm passed, she would figure out how to meet back up with Jason.

Sook-kyoung raced over to the remains of her horse. The front portion of the saddle was chewed up, and her rations and water were ruined. Miraculously, the anti-matter device had not been harmed thanks to the specially-designed saddle bag.

Ten feet from the carcass lay the gas mask she had been wearing. Picking it up and placing it on top of her head, and slinging the case holding the device over her shoulder, Sook-kyoung located the direction in which she had been heading and broke into a run.

JASON'S TEAM TRIED to maneuver around the three worms that towered in front of them. Most would have succeeded if the creatures had not bent their thoraxes at forty-five-degree angles and swept back and forth. Jason and Ustagov were knocked out of their saddles. One slammed into Slava's horse, tossing both animal and rider into the air.

A worm bent over Jason and lunged, its fang extended. The werehounds morphed into their demonic forms to protect their master. Lucifer jumped on top of Jason and arched his back as the worm's mouth closed around him, unable to penetrate the werehound's scales. Lucifer swayed back and forth, driving the three-inch spikes along his shoulders into the soft tissue. The worm shrieked, emitting a high-pitched muffled cry that came from deep in its throat, yet it refused to release its prey. Lilith circled around and jabbed her tail along its thorax, injecting the creature with paralyzing fluid. After several thrusts, the worm grew listless, yet still maintained its grip on Lucifer, the fangs desperately trying to pull him in.

Bringing her horse around to the side, Sasha slid out of her saddle and unsheathed her saber. Raising the weapon above her, she brought it down behind the worm's head. The blade cut into the slimy skin, creating a gash two feet deep. The worm let go of Lucifer and concentrated on Sasha. Because of the paralyzing fluid, its movements were sluggish. Sasha continued her attack, slicing two more deep wounds. When the creature opened its mouth to consume her, Sasha drove her saber into the soft tissue. Once the blade punctured the interior, she twisted her wrist, gouging out a chunk of tissue.

The creature shrieked and stood erect. As it tried to descend back into the ground, its thorax wobbled. The worm collapsed dead between Jason and Sasha, missing the former by inches.

Sasha rushed over and helped Jason to his feet. "Are you all right?"

"I've been banged around worse than this." Jason reached down and petted Lucifer on the head. Even in his demonic form, his tail wagged. "Forget about me. We have to protect the devices."

USTAGOV ATTEMPTED TO stand, stumbling forward onto his knees. Getting bowled over along with his horse had knocked the wind out of him worse than he realized. One of the worms slithered across the ground toward him, its extended prostomium having detected him. The doctor braced for the end, a part of him scientifically curious what it would be like to be eaten alive.

A sustained burst of automatic weapons fire lashed the worm's head. It stopped and shrieked, whipping its thorax back and forth to stave off the stinging. Haneef sat ten feet away on his horse, reloading his AK-47, while Jonah and Matthew stayed on either side of him to protect the device. Another burst of automatic weapons fire from the left punched into the creature. Jason and Sasha ran up on Ustagov's left, the latter helping the doctor to his feet.

"Come on." Jason reloaded and fired a three-round burst into the worm's head. "Grab your horse and let's get out of here."

"You don't have to tell me tw—"

The worm lunged again. Jason raised his AK-47 and emptied the rest of his magazine into its mouth as Haneef fired a broadside into the side of its head. With a screech of agony, the worm stiffened and disappeared into its crater.

"Now, while we have the chance."

Ustagov mounted his horse and headed in the direction of the dust storm. It was now five hundred feet away.

"WE'VE GOT PROBLEMS," said Antoine.

Jeanette stopped and spun her horse around toward the sound of gunfire. Half a mile away, the rest of the team fought the three worms. From this distance, it did not appear as if the battle was going well.

"We have to go back and help them," said Jeanette.

Antoine shook his head. "It won't do any good. The battle will be over by the time we get there."

"We have to do something," Vicky protested.

"We could provide a distraction," said Antoine. "Didn't the doctor say those things are attracted to vibrations?"

"He did." Jeanette slid out of her saddle. Antoine and Vicky joined her. As she stomped her feet against the ground, Jeanette wondered if this would work, and what they would do if they succeeded.

SLAVA LAY FACE down, dazed and with blurred vision. He heard shouting and automatic weapons fire. With the greatest of effort, he raised himself onto his hands and knees, and fell face first back on the dirt when the pain in his left arm caused the muscles to give out. When he opened his eyes, the ground beneath him spun. Slava squinted. Once the dizziness subsided, he pushed himself into a kneeling position using his right arm and opened his eyes again. One of the worms charged in his direction.

The worm did not attack Slava; it went after his horse, which had fallen beside him. The animal cried out as the fangs dug into its flanks. Slava reached out to the animal. A pair of hands grabbed him under his right arm and pulled him back. Luther leaned forward and said, "We have to get out of here."

"No." Slava pushed Luther away and headed back.

"You can't save him."

"I'm not trying to save the horse. The anti-matter device is attached to the saddle."

By now, the worm had devoured the horse up to its neck and had begun on its abdomen. Luther clutched the edge of the saddle and yanked while Slava struggled to unhitch the bag containing the device. Despite Luther's grip, each undulation of the fangs drew the horse deeper into the worm's mouth. The front part of the saddle was already being consumed. Slava worked frantically to release the bag. Just as he freed it, the worm thrust its thorax forward, knocking him and Luther onto the ground. The bag landed twenty feet from them. Slava rolled over and crawled after it.

"Watch out!"

The worm lowered its mouth toward Slava. The Russian rolled out of the way a moment before the creature's head slammed into the dirt beside him.

Luther unsheathed his broadsword and plunged the blade up to the hilt into the worm's flank, rotating the handle to maximize the wound. The worm jerked its head up, ripping the bladed weapon out of Luther's hands. Rather than disappear back into its crater, it lunged again, this time engulfing Luther down to his lower legs. It closed its mouth and raised its thorax upright. Luther's muffled screams could be heard from inside the worm. He frantically punched at the interior of its throat, stopping only when he slid past the creature's esophagus.

Slava got up and raced toward the saddle bag, scooping it as he ran past. He did not bother to look behind him, not wanting to know how close the worm was. Instead, every few seconds, he shifted direction, hoping to throw the creature off track. He felt a rumbling along the field's surface. The worm slithered across the earth directly behind him. Before Slava could change course, it collided with the Russian and knocked him to the ground. Slava clutched the bag against his chest so he would not lose it and attempted to roll out of the way. A sharp pain exploded down his legs. The worm's upper set of fangs had closed around his ankles and retracted, drawing him into its mouth. He cried out and tried to kick free, but his legs had been immobilized.

"Hang on!" Gabriel and Father Belsario rode up, dismounting before their horses came to a complete stop. The cleric knelt behind Slava, wrapped his arms underneath the Russian's shoulders, and pulled to prevent him from being devoured. Gabriel used his broadsword to attack the worm's head, hacking away chunks with each stroke. The creature ignored the assault, instead concentrating on its meal. The fangs undulated, the second set pulling Slava in deeper while the first closed around his knees. He screamed as the caps shattered under the weight. At that moment, the others rushed up. Jonah and Matthew protected Haneef and the anti-matter device; Jason and Ustagov fired three-round bursts from their AK-47s into the creature's neck, while Sasha stood opposite Gabriel, attacking the other side of the worm's head. The third set of fangs drew Slava in as the outer two opened and shifted position. When they did, Father Belsario yanked on Slava's shoulders, hoping to dislodge him. Instead, the first set of fangs bit down above the Russian's knees, tearing off his lower legs. Blood spurted across the dirt and the worm's head as Slava's arteries were severed. With no reason left to be careful of their shots, Jason and Ustagov switched to full automatic mode and fired thirty rounds into the creature. It bellowed a final shriek and collapsed.

Slinging his AK-47 over his shoulder, Jason rushed over to his friend. Father Belsario had laid Slava's shoulders on the ground. Jason held Slava's hand. "You're going to be okay."

Slava winced. "Thank God... you're a better leader... than a liar."

"I... I don't know what to say."

"There's nothing to say. I'm just glad—" Slava spasmed

and his eyes closed. Jason felt his wrist. The Russian had a weak pulse, and his breathing had increased to thirty breaths a minute. Slava opened his eyes again. "I'm just glad... I got to help... close the portals... in Russia."

"You did that, buddy." Jason squeezed Slava's hand. "Andre would have been proud."

"Andre... would have been proud... of *you*." Slava's breathing became fast and shallow, and his pulse barely perceptible. He slipped into unconsciousness. A moment later, Slava's life ebbed from his body. Father Belsario patted him on the shoulders and said a silent prayer over their fallen comrade. Jason wished his friend's soul a speedy journey to Heaven.

Sasha walked up beside Jason and placed her hand on his shoulder. "I hate to interrupt your grieving."

Jason followed her gaze. The dust storm had approached to within one hundred feet.

THE DISTRACTION CREATED by Jeanette and the others finally worked. The remaining worm detected the stomping and dived beneath the ground. She knew it headed toward them judging by the wave it created on the surface.

"What now?" Ian asked.

Jeanette checked her surroundings. The dust storm had closed to within two hundred feet on their left.

"Head into the storm," said Jeanette as she climbed into the saddle. "Once inside, slow down and stay close so we don't lose each other. Hopefully it won't find us."

The others mounted their horses and slid on their gas masks. When they were ready, Jeanette checked behind her. The worm approached rapidly, although still more than two hundred feet away.

Spurring her horse forward, Jeanette led her group into the dust storm.

JASON ATTACHED THE bag containing the anti-matter device to his saddle. He reached into another bag, withdrew a hundred-foot length of rope, and tied one end to his saddle. "There were some warehouses west of here. We're going to walk to them and wait out the storm there. Put on your masks and make sure your horses are ready." He passed the rope to Sasha.

She took it. "What's this for?"

"Loop this through the stirrups. That way we won't get separated. Now hurry."

Everyone worked as quickly as possible, finishing moments before the storm hit. The wind picked up, growing loud enough to drown out the nervous neighing of the horses, and throwing dirt and debris against their faceplates. When everyone was ready, Jason led the way through the dust.

SOOK-KYOUNG HAD BEEN jogging for several minutes when she paused to catch her breath. As she rested, she scanned the eastern horizon for anything that could offer protection. Sadly, she couldn't even spot a hillock or an abandoned vehicle. She would have to keep going and hopefully her luck would break good. By now, the leading edge of the storm had approached to within a hundred feet. Running would be useless. She placed her gas mask over her head, secured it, and started walking. The dust pounded against her back like hail.

A few minutes later, it engulfed Sook-kyoung completely, plunging her into darkness.

BOOK TWO

CHAPTER SEVENTEEN

J ASON WOKE TO the sounds of people chatting quietly, utensils clanking against metal plates, and horses milling about. He did not hear dust beating against the walls and ceiling. The last thing he remembered, the storm had been at its height and hammered the cement structure in full fury.

After being engulfed by the storm, Jason had led the team through the swirling cloud toward the buildings in the distance, coming across nothing for more than an hour. At first, he figured they had gotten lost. Finally, after close to ninety minutes of walking, a cement wall emerged from the dust, which turned out to be a garage for a local construction company. Jason had ordered the team to settle down and ride out the storm, and then rested his eyes for a few minutes to collect his thoughts. Considering that everyone else now ate dinner, he must have fallen asleep.

Rolling over, Jason bumped into a large brown mass. Lilith was curled up beside him. On feeling her master awake, she twisted her head to one side and licked Jason on the face. As he rubbed her belly, he sought out Lucifer. Sure enough, his faithful companion sat by Sasha at the fire, mooching food. Jason got to his feet and strolled over, with Lilith trotting beside him.

"Why didn't you wake me for dinner?"

"We tried," said Sasha. "You were sound asleep."

Haneef held up his tray. "And this is breakfast."

"I slept all night?"

"You needed it," said Sasha. "Besides, the storm didn't let

up until early in the morning. It's not like we were going anywhere."

"Has anybody been outside?"

Haneef shook his head. "Not yet. The sun only came up a few minutes ago."

Jason grabbed his binoculars and made his way to one of the garage bays. As he raised the metal door, a seven-inch pile of sand and dust that had drifted against it collapsed onto his feet. He stepped out and surveyed the landscape.

Dust and sand covered everything, making the area appear like a dirty gray winter setting. He raised the binoculars to his eyes and scanned the horizon. Several miles away, he spotted two large and one small mounds of dust, the remains of the slaughtered worms and his friend Slava. He saw no signs of the missing team members. His own team's footprints to the garage had been wiped clean by the wind, so tracking the others would be impossible.

Sasha moved up beside Jason and handed him a tin cup of coffee. "I thought you might want this."

"Thanks." He lowered the binoculars and took the cup. When he did, pain shot through his wounded shoulder. He noticed fresh blood on his flight suit. "Shit. Did I reopen it during combat?"

"No. You banged it around so much it bled a little. Ustagov checked it while you were out."

"I slept through that, too?"

Sasha nodded and motioned to the field. "Any sign of the others?"

"Not a thing," Jason answered. "The last I saw them, they were about a mile to our south when we were running from the worms. Then we were attacked and the storm hit. I have no idea what happened to them or which way they went."

"I'm sorry."

"There's nothing for you to be sorry about. Come on. I need to talk to the team."

Jason and Sasha rejoined the others and sat down around the fire.

"Are we heading out to search for the rest of our people?" Haneef asked.

"No." Jason reached out and patted Lucifer. "It's their responsibility to backtrack and find us."

"Do you really mean that?"

"I do." Jason stopped the others before anyone could speak. "I know it sounds uncaring, but I have no choice. We lost eight people yesterday, and at least one of those worms is still out there. If we go traipsing through the countryside, we might lose more people trying to find the rest of the team who are probably dead already."

"We have to try at least," Haneef protested.

"I agree," added Sasha. "We don't stand much of a chance of closing the portal without them."

"We stand even less of a chance if we go searching for them. Remember, we're on our own in China, and if we keep losing people at this rate, our expedition ends here. I'm not going to let that happen. We still have two of the devices, and we know the third is not far from here. Father Belsario and I will head out after breakfast, retrieve Sook-kyoung's device, and give her and Slava a proper burial. The rest of you stay put. Set up a beacon fire and post a guard. Hopefully, if the others are nearby, they'll find us. We can only give them twenty-four hours. After that, if they're not back, we move on."

"Jeanette is missing," said Sasha.

"That's irrelevant. She knew what the risks were when she joined us and how slim were the chances of survival."

"It's not fair."

"I'm not making my decisions based on what's fair. I'm making them based on what's necessary to complete our goal."

"Jason's right," Father Belsario interrupted. "Every one of us is expendable. Sasha, you realize that more than anyone."

"I know." Sasha lowered her head.

"I would make only one change in your plan," said the cleric. "Let me and Gabriel retrieve the device and bury the bodies. If something happens to us, we'll be resurrected in a few days. Your death is permanent and irreplaceable."

"You're right, but I'm still going with you."

"It's not necessary."

"It is to me."

Father Belsario nodded, understanding what Jason meant.

Jason asked Matthew, "Will you build a fire on the roof and keep the first watch for the others?"

"Of course."

"Thank you. Haneef, after breakfast take an inventory of what supplies we have left so we know how to ration them. Since Vicky and Sook-kyoung used to take care of the horses, Sasha and Ustagov will now do it. Are there any questions?"

No one had any.

"You hold the fort here. Father Belsario, Gabriel, and I will head out to get the other device."

A pair of whimpers sounded to Jason's left. Lucifer and Lilith stared up at him with their soulful eyes. "Yes, you can come, too."

The wagging of tails indicated the werehounds approved of his plan.

CHAPTER EIGHTEEN

"**I**T'S SUNRISE," SAID Antoine. "What do you want to do?"

"I'm not sure yet." Jeanette leaned against a tree and stared into the woods. She honestly had no clue what their course of action should be. As pissed off as Jeanette was at Jason, she desperately wished he was here now. He would be able to figure out the next move.

The worm had broken off its pursuit of Jeanette's group after they had entered the dust storm, probably because Ustagov had been correct about the creature not being able to detect their movements with so much noise being generated along the ground. They had eventually reached the woods and continued for another few miles to put as much distance as possible between them and the creature. Being amongst the trees had the added benefit of dissipating much of the wind's intensity. Once night had fallen, they had settled down in their sleeping bags until the storm had passed. When it did, Jeanette set up a campfire and tried to get her bearings.

That was more difficult than she originally thought. Jeanette had no idea how far they had ridden and in which direction. With the storm having covered their tracks, she had no way of retracing their movements. She had a general idea where Jason and the others might be based on his last known position. However, that assumed he had not moved since then, which seemed unlikely. She had three options. She could stay put and wait for Jason's team to find them; there were too many variables attached to that, key among them that the others could spend days searching for her group, expending valuable time that could be used to close the portal. Jeanette could go searching for the others, but that could also take days and had no guarantee of success. That left only one viable alternative.

Jeanette pushed herself off the tree and faced the rest of her group. "We're going to head south and find the portal."

"Shouldn't we wait for Jason?" Vicky asked tentatively.

"We have no idea how long it'll take them to find us, or if they'll be successful."

"Or if they're even looking," said Ian.

Jeanette did not want to entertain that possibility. "We were circling back to the G1 when the worms attacked, so it's a safe bet that the rest of the group will continue doing the same. We'll head southwest until we reach the road and proceed to Shenyang. If Jason does the same, we'll eventually meet back up."

"We don't have any of the devices," said Antoine. "What will we do if we discover the portal?"

"Once we know where it is, we'll find Jason and the others and lead them to it."

"And what if we never find him?"

Vicky reached over and punched Antoine in the shoulder. He glared at the woman, more hurt than angry.

"I know it's not the best option," began Jeanette. "If any of you have a better idea, I'm willing to listen."

Jeanette hoped one of them would, but they did not.

"Grab something to eat and get the horses ready. We move out in half an hour."

As the others followed orders, Jeanette stared back through the trees. What Antoine had said bothered her, although he did not mean to upset her. She had not considered the reality of the situation until then. They had lost Sook-kyoung and her device. If something had happened to Haneef and Slava, they had failed. They had come all this way for nothing. And if something had happened to Jason—

Jeanette refused to consider that scenario, yet she could not get the idea out of her head. She wished she had treated Jason better this past week. Not that it mattered. She would make it up to him once they were together again. Somehow Jeanette knew he was alive, as if she could feel him nearby. And she knew he would do everything possible to find her.

CHAPTER NINETEEN

SOOK-KYOUNG WOKE WITH a start and opened her eyes. She saw only the dirt and sand that covered her. Panic set in. She gasped but took in plenty of oxygen because of her gas mask. Sook-kyoung realized her erratic breathing resulted from anxiety. Taking a deep breath, she held it for several seconds, which calmed her nerves.

The events of last night slowly came back. When the dust storm had engulfed her, she had continued walking west toward the G1. Trudging through the wind and dust had tired her out, and when she eventually tripped and fell, she had laid there until sleep overtook her. She had no idea how long she had been out; however, considering the layer of sand that covered her, it probably had been a while. Pushing herself up, Sook-kyoung felt the earth cascade off her body, creating a small cloud as it hit the ground. She rested on her knees a moment, unable to hear anything or see out of the faceplate of her gas mask. Closing her eyes, she pulled off the mask and shook her head. Sand slid across her brow and cheeks and dislodged from her ears. The storm had stopped. The fresh air felt good in her lungs, as did the warm sunshine against her skin. She opened her eyes.

A dozen Chinese men formed a semi-circle in front of Sook-kyoung, each armed with a bow and arrow. One stood three feet away, staring down at her through a pair of Ray-Bans. Sook-kyoung grabbed her AK-47. The men with bows raised their weapons and aimed.

Ray-Ban held up his hand and spoke in Mandarin. The

bowmen hesitated then lowered their weapons and kept their fingers on the nocks of the arrows, ready to fire quickly if necessary. Ray-Ban focused his attention back to Sook-kyoung and removed his sunglasses. His brown eyes were soulful, yet cold and hardened by everything he had witnessed over the last year. Sook-kyoung saw nothing threatening in them. She slowly placed her automatic weapon back on the ground.

Ray-Ban nodded. He spoke to her in Korean laden with a thick Mandarin accent. "My name is Qiang."

"I'm Sook-kyoung."

"Don't be afraid. We're here to help you. Are you all right?"

Sook-kyoung ran her fingers through her ponytail, dislodging sand and dirt. "I'm a little shaken up after getting caught in that storm yesterday, but other than that I'm fine."

"Good. We'll take you back to our camp where you can rest up and get a hot meal." Qiang offered her his hand. Sook-kyoung took it and he helped her to her feet. "First, we should find your friends and make certain they're okay."

"I don't know who you're talking about," Sook-kyoung lied. "I'm alone."

The friendliness drained from Qiang's expression. "I'm sorry to hear you say that."

"Why?"

"Because we've been following your group since Harbin and thought we could trust you."

"You can."

"Lying does not equate with trust. We'll take you back to camp and deal with you later."

"I don't want to be a bother." Sook-kyoung picked up the saddle bag with the anti-matter device and her personal bag, slinging them over her left shoulder. "I'll be on my way. I appreciate the offer, though."

"It's not an offer." Qiang snapped his fingers. Two of his men stepped forward. One took the bags from Sook-kyoung, the other picked up her AK-47. They moved back in line. "Will you please come with us?"

"Do I have a choice?"

"Yes. You can go peacefully or we can force you."

Sook-kyoung shrugged her shoulders and began walking.

CHAPTER TWENTY

J ASON, FATHER BELSARIO, and Gabriel stood by the partially-devoured remains of Gaston's horse which they had dug out from under a mound of sand. Lucifer and Lilith sniffed the ground around the carcass, the latter pawing the horse to see if it was alive. Jason moved away from the others, strolling in a circle fifty feet from the remains. When he again approached the Purgatoriati, he stopped.

"Isn't this where the worms killed Gaston and Sook-kyoung?"

The cleric nodded.

"Where is she?"

"Maybe the last worm came back and ate her."

"Why didn't it also take the horse?"

"I don't know."

"Maybe the demons prefer fresh kill," suggested Gabriel.

Jason thought for a moment. "Shit."

"What?"

"What if Sook-kyoung wasn't dead?"

"She took a direct hit by the worm. I doubt she could have survived that."

"We never checked." Jason paced back and forth. He couldn't believe how stupid... no, how insensitive he had been. Sook-kyoung had been a valuable team member from day one and deserved better than to be left behind.

Father Belsario placed a comforting hand on Jason's shoulder. "Don't be hard on yourself. You know as well as any of us that we would have lost several people if we tried to go back for her. You did what you had to do."

"That doesn't make it any easier."

"If Sook-kyoung is alive, we'll find her."

Lilith sniffed the spot.

"Do you have her scent, girl?"

The werehound continued sniffing.

Jason frowned. "The storm must have covered her tracks."

"I can go search," Gabriel volunteered. "If I find her, we can catch up with you later."

"We can't afford to lose anyone else. If she's alive, she'll make her way toward Shenyang, probably along the G1. If we're lucky, we'll all be back together in a few days."

"God willing."

"Come on." Jason headed back to the garage. "I want to make sure we have enough time to give Slava a decent burial and get back before sunset."

CHAPTER TWENTY-ONE

"**D**OES ANYONE HAVE any idea where we are?" Jeanette asked.

"We're bloody lost, mate." Ian thought he had said it under his breath. Jeanette had heard him.

"That's not very helpful."

"Sorry."

Jeanette felt bad for snapping at Ian, although right now she was in no mood to apologize. In truth, they were "bloody lost" because of her.

They had broken camp and headed southeast. Several hours passed before they picked up the G1 and proceeded towards Shenyang. Not until a few hours later did Jeanette realize they were, in fact, on the G25 and approaching a town called Kangping thirty-five miles away. Without a map, that information was useless. Jeanette had opted to continue until they could get their bearings. She had not counted on traveling another two hours with no clue as to their whereabouts.

Antoine brought his horse alongside Jeanette.

"Are you going to tell me we're lost?" she asked.

The Moroccan scrunched his eyebrows. "Why would I tell you the obvious?"

"Sorry."

"I wanted to show you that." He pointed ahead of them.

Two hundred feet in front of them off to the side of the road stood a rural Chinese version of a highway rest stop. Two tractor trailers, three smaller trucks, and half a dozen run-down cars lay scattered across the parking lot. Three structures were bunched together. Off to the left stood a small concrete building with two doors, the one on the right marked with a female figure and the one on the left with a male. Off to the right stood a small convenience stand long ago picked clean. Jeanette's interest focused on the structure in the center—a wooden wall covered with a green-tiled roof that mounted a glass display. She spurred her horse ahead. The others followed.

"Yes!" Jeanette said aloud when she pulled her horse up to the display wall. A map was pinned to the interior corkboard. The group dismounted and tied their horses to the bumper of one of the tractor trailers. Jeanette used the sleeve of her winter coat to wipe away the accumulated dirt and grime from the glass, then she and Vicky checked out the map. Antoine stayed close by, unslinging his AK-47 in case of an ambush. Ian rushed off toward the restroom.

As luck should have it, the map had the names of the local town and cities printed in English beneath the Chinese characters. The women studied it, and Jeanette cursed under her breath. The G25 split off from the G1 five miles south of Siping and headed southwest at a forty-five-degree angle. According to a red star on the map, the "You are here" marker, they were halfway between the villages of Cilushuzhen and Simianchengzhen, ten miles west of the G1.

Jeanette sighed.

"It's okay," said Vicky.

"It's going to take half a day for us to get back on course."

"At least we know where we are and how to correct it."

Jeanette tried to open the outer lid of the display case, only to find it locked. Removing her bayonet, she placed the tip of the blade in the lock and fumbled with it.

Antoine stepped up. "Let me get that."

Jeanette stepped aside. Antoine raised his elbow and smashed the glass, then used the stock of his AK-47 to clear away the remaining shards. Jeanette reached in and removed the map.

"Should we start heading west?" Vicky asked.

"It's too late. I want to make sure we have a secure location for the night."

Antoine pointed to the restrooms. "What about those. They're sturdy and no one can get in."

"No one would want to," said Ian as he returned from the stalls. "Those things have been festering since the apocalypse. You don't want to go in there."

Vicky motioned ahead of them. "There are a bunch of buildings further down the road. One is a service station. I'm sure we can find a place to hole up there for the night."

"Sounds good to me." Jeanette walked back to the horses. "Let's get moving before the sun goes down."

FROM THE SADDLE of his horse, Hong watched through binoculars as Jeanette and her group exited the rest stop.

"That's them," said Deng. "The ones who arrived in Harbin. They must be the only survivors from the worm attack."

"Or they became separated from the others during the dust storm."

"That's possible, too, I guess." Deng paused. "Do you want to contact them?"

Hong weighed his options. After they had lost the outsiders' trail in the dust storm, Qiang had dispatched search parties to locate them again and, if possible, introduce themselves to determine if they posed a threat. His people were in no danger since they outnumbered the outsiders three-to-one. Still, approaching them with horse-mounted troops might accidentally precipitate the encounter he wanted to avoid. Plus, he had no idea of the location of the rest of their group, or if they were still alive. Usually a man of action, this time Hong felt playing it safe was the best option.

Deng asked again. "Do you want to contact them?"

"Not yet." Hong maneuvered his horse to face Deng. "Take two of the men and go back to Qiang. Tell him we found some of the outsiders and they're still heading for Shenyang. Ask him what he wants us to do. We'll follow the outsiders and see what they're up to."

"Of course." Deng gathered two horsemen and rode off.

Hong turned to his second in command, Xiao-ping. "Tell the others we're going to follow the outsiders, but to keep a safe distance. I don't want them to know we're here until we get orders from Qiang."

CHAPTER TWENTY-TWO

THE NEXT MORNING, Jason stood outside the door to the garage, the werehounds curled up at his feet. He finished his coffee, long since gone cold, as he scanned the horizon, hoping Sook-kyoung or Jeanette's group would appear. He hated the idea of leaving, yet he had no choice. The longer he stayed, the more time the demons had to reinforce the portal and prepare for their arrival. Jason could only pray the others had survived the dust storm and the worm attack and had followed the original plan. If so, the chances were good he would catch up with them.

Father Belsario joined Jason. "Everyone is ready to go."

"Thanks." Jason poured the rest of his tepid coffee into the dirt and flipped the tin cup several times to flick out any residue.

"Are you sure you don't want me to keep Matthew and Gabriel here for a few days?"

"I took care of that." Jason motioned to the two open cans of red paint and the paintbrush that lay beside the door. "Besides, I have to assume we lost the others for good, so I need all hands on deck if we hope to close the portal."

"I understand."

Ten minutes later, the horses were saddled and packed, and the remainder of the team ready to depart. One by one they left the warehouse, with Jason in the lead, flanked by Lilith and Lucifer who constantly ran ahead to sniff for potential danger. They made their way east toward the main road. When five hundred feet from the structure, Jason checked on the message he had painted on the garage wall.

> Jeanette, Sook-kyoung
> We're heading to Shenyang along the G1
> Catch up with us there

CHAPTER TWENTY-THREE

"**A**RE YOU SURE we're going in the right direction?" Jeanette asked.

"According to the map we got from the rest stop, we are," Ian answered.

"We should have reached the G1 by now."

"Don't worry about it, mate. The two roads are at an angle to each other. We'll get there soon enough." Ian pointed to a hill off to their left. "Let's head that way. Maybe we can get our bearings from up there."

Jeanette maneuvered her horse toward the hill. Ian was right. They had only been traveling a few hours, barely enough time to reach the G1. However, that did little to assuage her nervousness. Part of her anxiety involved being separated from Jason. She realized how much she cared for him, and how her jealousy over Sasha had jeopardized their relationship; she wanted to work things out between them. Another major stress factor was being isolated from the others. Jeanette did not worry about encountering any Demon Spawn because her people could handle themselves in a fight, especially Antoine. However, her group had limited food and water and only ten magazines of ammunition to share amongst them. If they did not meet up with the others within the next day or two, or at least find food and water along the way, their supplies would run out and they would be living on borrowed time. As they crested the hill, Jeanette told herself everything would be fine.

To Jeanette's surprise, a caravan lay spread out at the foot of the opposite slope. Her body tensed as she went into fight-or-flight mode, remembering their last encounter at the walled town a few days earlier. She relaxed, however, because these people seemed docile and posed little threat. Raising her binoculars, she studied the site. Five farm utility wagons and a school bus rigged to be pulled by horses formed a semi-circle around the main camp where a dozen tents had been erected. Jeanette estimated approximately one hundred people, a third of them women and children, populated the makeshift compound. A group hung clothes to dry along a rope that stretched between the bus and one of the wagons. A man had set up an anvil by a fire pit and shoed horses. Others did various chores while the smaller children played on another wagon. Jeanette searched specifically for armed guards or manned gun emplacements but could not observe any. Even though a few of the men and women wore side arms, and Type 63 automatic rifles were stacked in teepee-like formations at various locations throughout the compound, no one seemed overly concerned about security.

"They've spotted us," said Vicky. "Over there, by the school bus."

Jeanette swung the binoculars in that direction. Sure enough, half a dozen kids stared and pointed. The adults soon joined in. No one went for their weapons. A young woman made her way across the compound to the base of the hill and waved. Jeanette lowered her binoculars and waved back. The woman motioned for them to join her.

"What do you think?" Vicky asked. "Should we go down?"

"They out gun us," offered Ian.

Antoine shook his head. "If they were a threat, they would have fired on us by now."

"If we run, we appear weak," said Jeanette. "Maybe they can share some food and water, and hopefully give us information on the location of the portal. Stay on guard, though. If they try anything, we get out as fast as possible."

"Sounds good to me," said Antoine.

The others concurred.

"Then let's do this." Jeanette led her group down the slope.

The young woman who had invited them smiled as they approached. Attractive and well-groomed, she wore clean leather pants, a white shirt, and a tan leather jacket. Her raven black hair hung past her shoulders and framed a face pretty enough to belong to a model. The woman's deep brown eyes were warm and welcoming. She stepped up to Jeanette and offered her hand.

"*Dobro pozhalovat' v nash lager'. Pozhaluysta, vkhodite i chuvstvuyte sebya kak doma.*"

Jeanette shook her hand. "I'm sorry. I don't speak Russian."

"You speak English."

"Yes."

"Excellent. My name is Mei."

"I'm Jeanette." She introduced the others.

"It's a pleasure to meet you all." Mei stepped back and gestured toward the compound. "Welcome to our camp."

"What about our weapons?" Antoine asked.

"Given what the world is like today, I wouldn't ask you to give them up. I only ask that you don't make us regret our generosity." Mei moved toward the tents. "Come inside and rest."

Jeanette and the others dismounted, took their horses' reins, and followed Mei.

"How do you know so many languages?" Jeanette asked.

"I studied linguistics at the Beijing Foreign Studies University. I speak six languages. My father used to chastise me about wasting my time, telling me I would be better off studying medicine or science. I'd like to think he'd be proud of me now."

As they walked through the camp, people stopped what they were doing to watch the newcomers. Some stared suspiciously; most nodded a welcome. A few of the younger children ran up and waved, while others fell in behind Antoine and gaped at him.

Mei shoed them away. "Please forgive them. They've never met someone so big, or someone who is African-American."

"That's okay." When two of the boys snuck back, Antoine spun around with a huge grin on his face and growled. The boys screamed and ran off, laughing. "I'm not from America, though. I'm from Morocco."

"Are you all from Morocco?"

"No," said Jeanette, phrasing her answer carefully. "We're originally from France."

"You're a long way from home. Why are you here in China?"

"We're looking for a safe place to settle down."

"I can relate. I'd hate to think what my life would be like if not for the friends I made here." Mei leaned closer to Jeanette. "We've heard rumors that things are bad in France and Russia, and that someone is trying to close the portals."

"We've heard the same thing, which is why we've kept traveling east."

"Well, you're safe now." Mei stopped in front of a tent and pulled aside the flap, motioning for them to enter. It contained a rolled up sleeping bag and a backpack. Mei grabbed the items and hefted them onto her shoulder. "This is my tent. You can use it."

"We don't want to impose."

"You're not imposing. I'll sleep with some of the other girls for a few days. You can tie up your horses in the back. I'll make sure they're fed. Get some rest. I'll have one of the children come for you when dinner is ready. If you need anything, let me know."

Mei exited the tent and closed the flap behind her. Antoine waited a few seconds before he strolled over and opened it again. "We're clear."

"What do you make of that?" Vicky asked.

Jeanette shrugged. "They appear friendly enough."

Antoine stepped back to the group. "I noticed you were vague in your answers."

"The less they know about us the better, at least until we know more about them."

"Agreed," said Ian. Antoine nodded.

"Maybe we lucked out like we did in Russia and have run across a group who can help us. It's too early to tell yet."

"What do we do in the meantime?" Vicky asked.

"Stay alert and play it cool. Tonight, at dinner, I'm going to find how much Mei really knows about what's going on here in China."

CHAPTER TWENTY-FOUR

DINNER WAS PLAIN yet filling. The cooks had prepared vegetables and rice, with hot tea to drink. Everyone stood in line, received their portion into one of two tin cups, and gathered in small groups near the center of the compound where they patiently waited. Once the last person had received their share and sat down, Mei led the group in blessings in Mandarin. Jeanette did not understand the words although she recognized the cadence as belonging to The Lord's Prayer. With grace concluded, everyone began to eat. When they were well into the meal, Jeanette struck up a conversation.

"How long have you been here?"

Mei was confused. "I was born and raised in China."

"I mean, how did you all come together after the portal opened?"

"Ah, you mean after the End of Godlessness." Mei placed down her tin cup. "Everyone has a different story. We survived those first few weeks of what you westerners would call the End of Days and eventually came together under the single cause. For example, my mother lived in Changchun, so I attempted to travel to be with her. Unfortunately, I only made it as far as Shenyang before I could go no further. I wandered aimlessly for months, trying to survive on what little food remained and avoiding the gangs, until Bai found me and took me in."

"How come the area isn't swarming with Demon Spawn?" Ian asked.

Mei crinkled her eyebrows. "Demon Spawn?"

"The things that came through the portal," Jeanette clarified.

"We call them *láizì míngjiè*, which you would translate as 'those from the Underworld'. In the beginning, they swarmed across northeast China, especially the soulless hordes. That's why there are so few people around. Those who weren't killed ran away. Many headed to Beijing or farther south. Those in the north fled west to Mongolia or east toward Vladivostok."

"What happened to those from the Underworld?" Vicky asked.

"Bai got rid of them."

That was the second time Jeanette had heard the name tonight. "Who's Bai?"

"She's the one we follow." Mei spread her arms. "She made it so that we can live again without fear."

"Is she here now?"

"No." Mei picked up her tin cup and resumed eating. "We're going to meet up with her in a few days."

Jeanette took a chance and asked the question most on her mind. "Is the portal nearby?"

"The what?"

"The portal to the Underworld."

Mei suddenly understood and nodded. "Yes, it's located just north of Shenyang, only a few days' ride."

Jeanette attempted to contain her excitement. "I have a map. Can you point out its location?"

"We can take you there."

"I don't want to put you in danger."

Mei brushed away the concerns with a wave of her hand. "It's no danger to us. We check on its status every few weeks. In fact, we're heading that way tomorrow morning."

"I don't want to be a bother."

"You're not a bother." Mei reached out and patted Jeanette's hand. "Follow us and we'll show you exactly how to get there. We just need to stop by another village first. Is that okay?"

Jeanette would have preferred to be told the location so she could find it herself. That way, she could stay in the area and search for Jason and the others. However, she did not want to offend her hosts and squander the opportunity. The others nodded in approval.

"That's fine," said Jeanette. "We appreciate you doing this for us."

"It's our pleasure. We'll take good care of you."

CHAPTER TWENTY-FIUE

J ASON ATE ONLY half his MRE and shared the rest with Lilith and Lucifer. He had been so distracted the past two days that he did not have much of an appetite and survived mostly on caffeine, which did more harm than good. He took his tin cup to the fence of the stable they had spent the night in and stared out over the countryside. Lilith followed, leaving her mate behind to beg for more breakfast.

As hard as Jason tried to focus on the task at hand, his mind kept going back to the missing team members. Death had become so commonplace in this world he had become inured to it. Still, potentially losing eight people in one day was tough, both emotionally and strategically. With regards to Jeanette, he did not know what bothered him more, the fact that he might never see her again or that they had left so many issues unresolved. On top of that, Jason felt ashamed that he had not checked on Sook-kyoung after the attack by the giant worms and took for granted that she had been killed. Lesson learned. In the future, no one gets left behind under any circumstances.

Weighing on Jason's mind as much as his missing friends was the loss of the anti-matter device. The twin portals in Russia had forced them to use their spare, eliminating any margin of error. If he could not retrieve the one Sook-kyoung had been carrying, then they would not be able to close all the portals and their expedition would have been for nothing. A possibility existed that another means had been found to close the portals, even though the chances of that were slim. If someone had developed such a method, why hadn't they used it? Jason had to face the realization that all the time his team had spent on the road from Mont St. Michel to northeast China, and all the lives sacrificed along the way, had been for nothing. They would have failed. That's not true. *He* would have failed.

In any case, nothing would ever get accomplished if he stood around whining about how things had panned out. Jason guzzled the last of his coffee and headed back to the stables. The others had finished breakfast and were packing to leave. Jason tracked down Ustagov.

"Where are we now?"

"Let's check." The doctor removed the map and spread it out along the wall. He held up one end while Jason held the other. Ustagov ran his index finger across the surface for a few seconds before stopping and pressing it against the paper. "We're here, near Changtu."

"How long before we get to Shenyang?"

"If we keep this pace, it should be another four days." Ustagov refolded the map. "Of course, that's if the portal is in or near Shenyang."

"It's all we have to go on for now. Hopefully as we get closer—"

"Excuse me." Sasha stepped up to the two men. "Jason, you need to see this."

They headed outside where the others stood by the fence. A dozen horses came up the G1 from the south, left the road, and approached the stable. The four horsemen in the lead each carried bows and quivers of arrows, keeping the weapons draped across their shoulders so that they posed no imminent threat. The remaining horseman stayed farther to the rear. Jason wanted to play it safe.

"Are your people still on perimeter watch?" Jason asked Father Belsario.

"Yes."

"Keep them there in case this is a diversion." He spoke

louder so the others could hear. "Father Belsario, Haneef, and I will meet them. The rest of you cover us. Don't raise your weapons or fire unless they do so first. If they try anything, take them down."

"You got it," said Ustagov.

Jason patted Lucifer and Lilith. "Stay here."

The two werehounds whimpered but obeyed.

Jason opened the gate to the fence and headed out to greet the horsemen. Father Belsario stayed several paces behind on his left with Haneef on his right. Jason and Haneef kept their AK-47s slung over their shoulders. Father Belsario draped her cloak over the handle of his broadsword. When the two groups were fifty feet apart, Jason stopped and held up his hands.

"That's close enough."

The horsemen halted. The apparent leader of the group, who wore Ray-Bans, spread his arms beside him with his hands facing Jason. "I mean you no harm."

"So far we haven't met anyone in this region who has been friendly to us."

"Sadly, no one trusts each other in China anymore."

"Then you understand what I'm talking about."

"My name is Qiang." He spurred his horse forward and slowly approached Jason, his right hand outstretched.

"I said that's close enough."

Qiang stopped short. His expression became angry and insulted.

From the rear of the horsemen a familiar voice cried out, "Jason, it's okay."

A horse moved from the back of the group and circled around. Sook-kyoung rode in the saddle, with the saddle bag containing the missing anti-matter device draped beside her leg. She looked tired and haggard; most of them probably did. Sook-kyoung stopped in front of Jason.

"Qiang's people found me two days ago and have been taking care of me. They're friendly and they have the same goal we do."

"That's true," added Qiang, his good nature having returned. "Our purpose is to close the… what do you call it? Oh yes, the portal."

"You know where it is?" Jason asked.

Qiang nodded. "We've been trying to shut it since it opened, but without success. Sook-kyoung says you have a way to succeed where we failed."

"I trust them," said Sook-kyoung. "You should, too."

Jason met her gaze, studying it for any indication of fear, lying, or coercion. Instead, Sook-kyoung's eyes pleaded with him to believe her. He used his sixth sense to scan for negative auras, either from her or the horsemen. He detected nothing malignant. Jason stepped over to Sook-kyoung.

"Are you sure about this?"

She nodded.

Closing the gap with Qiang, Jason extended his hand. Qiang leaned over in his saddle and gave it a firm pump.

"My name's Jason. Forgive me if I'm a little paranoid."

"Everybody in China has to be cautious these days. It's hard to know who's a friend and who's an enemy."

"Qiang has a lot to fill you in on," added Sook-kyoung.

"My camp is a few miles from here," said Qiang. "It's in a safer location and is better defended. We should go there to talk."

"Why can't we stay here?"

"Jason," said Sook-kyoung. "Trust Qiang on this. You have no idea how big of a shit storm we've walked into."

CHAPTER TWENTY-SIX

M EI'S PEOPLE HAD broken camp right after breakfast, including the tent Jeanette and her group stayed in. It had taken less than fifteen minutes to get ready to move out, and the Demon Hunters waited for the larger group to get underway.

Antoine moved up alongside of Jeanette. "Are you still planning on going with them?"

"They're the only ones who know where the portal is. Once we do, we can find the others and lead them to it."

"They could point it out to us on a map."

"They're just gung-ho about being hospitable."

Antoine leaned close, so no one could hear him. "Don't you find these people strange?"

"Of course. They're as odd as a three-franc note. They've been through a lot. After spending so many months in the field, I bet we'd seem odd to the folks back home."

"These people give me the creeps."

"I can't argue with you on that." Jeanette faced Antoine. "I'll tell you what. If we start getting negative feelings about these people, we'll go our own way. In the meantime, I'll chat with Mei and see if she'll tell me where the portal is. Does that sound okay?"

"A little bit." Antoine did not sound completely convinced.

Mei walked up to the group and slid her hands around Jeanette's. "Are you still coming with us?"

"We planned to."

"Perfect." Mei squeezed lovingly and let go. "Follow us. We

have to make a quick stop a few hours from here, and then we'll take you to the gate."

"Thanks."

Five minutes later, the caravan departed and headed south-east.

CHAPTER TWENTY-SEVEN

Q IANG WAS CORRECT about his compound being better defended. His people had established themselves in what once had been an illegal steel mill hastily erected in the countryside. A ten-foot-high concrete wall cordoned off several hundred acres of land. Beyond the barrier, thirteen smoke-stacks and cooling towers dotted the skyline. Immense piles of coal and stone channeled the horsemen toward the wall until they eventually emerged into a one-hundred-foot-wide clearing. An old school bus, its yellow paint long since faded and the exposed metal surfaces rusted, blocked the entrance from the inside. Upon spotting Qiang, a woman in a makeshift guard tower mounted on top of the wall shouted to someone below. Seconds later, three men rolled the school bus across the entrance, allowing the returnees to enter, then pushed the vehicle back across the opening.

The inside of the compound appeared less accommodating than the surrounding countryside. A few large structures dotted the area, most either made of poorly-poured concrete or corroded corrugated iron walls. Not far from the entrance, a dilapidated trailer that once served as an office had been converted into a chicken coop. Rivulets of steel wound their way through the compound where molten overflows had haphazardly coursed. The current occupants had attempted to clean up the factory as much as possible, pushing garbage, debris, and old machinery into the many cooling pits that pocked the landscape to get them out of sight. It did little to help. Soot and grime covered everything, and not a tree or blade of grass were visible. The Chinese had gouged out this portion of the land and not even time would be able to restore it.

As they made their way through camp, Jason observed guards in makeshift towers along the walls every two hundred feet, plus another fifty mounted horsemen, each armed with a bow and arrow, and as many camp followers. A dozen horsemen conducted target practice in an open area bordered on three sides by parked trucks. One by one, they rode at full gallop past stacked bales of hay with a circular piece of cloth one foot in diameter attached. With few exceptions, all the arrows struck the cloth, even at distances of one hundred feet.

"Your archery skills are impressive," said Jason.

"Thank you," Qiang replied. "We had to become skilled bowmen by necessity. Guns were outlawed in China under the Communists. After the End of Days, there were very few weapons for people to defend themselves, and those that were available ran out of ammunition quickly. Bows had the advantage that they were easy to make, and after a battle you can retrieve your arrows. You can't do that with bullets."

Ustagov made his way to the head of the line. "You adopted the Mongolian horse archery tactics perfected by Genghis Khan."

"It was the only standard we had to go by," Qiang replied. "It took us months before we got anywhere near as good as we are now. That's why our enemies refer to us at the *Xiongnu*."

"*Xiongnu?*"

"It's the name of the ancient horsemen who came from Mongolia."

"And who are your enemies?"

"They're not just our enemy. They're the enemy of everyone in north China. If you're here to destroy the *mén qù jiùshú*, then they're your enemy as well."

"*Mén qù jiùshú?*" Ustagov asked.

"That's the Sataners' name for it. What you would call the

'Gate to Salvation'." Qiang pointed to a structure made of corrugated steel in the center of the compound. "I'll explain everything once we get inside."

Ten minutes later, Qiang and Jason's people were seated on worn pillows that had experienced better days and were being served tea in plastic cups by some of the camp's women. When the ladies left, Qiang began his explanation.

"When the gate opened north of Shenyang, most Chinese thought little about it. We assumed the government would take care of it, which they did. Well, they tried to. The People's Liberation Army was no match for those from the Underworld. For the first few weeks, the battles were fierce. The PLA had some early success, but they could not control the number of demons coming through. Rumors spread that Beijing planned to use nuclear weapons to blast the gate out of existence but decided against it after what happened in Moscow. After three weeks of fighting, Beijing withdrew its military and left north China to its fate. That's when the Sataners formed. They feel China is being punished for forsaking God and embracing Communism, and that God no longer cares. They don't view the opening of the gate as something disastrous, but as a harbinger of their impending salvation. To save themselves, the Sataners made a deal with Satan."

"That must have worked out well for them," chuckled Sasha.

"Actually, it did. An arrangement was reached in which Hell regulated the number of demons coming through."

"You're joking." Father Belsario sounded incredulous.

Qiang shook his head. "Hordes of soulless wanderers used to walk the land, plus every other monstrosity the Underworld had to offer. Some made it as far north as Harbin and to the Korean Peninsula. Hell pulled back most of its demons and keeps them close to the gate to protect it. All except the giant insects, which have a mind of their own. Those creatures still roam at will, which you found out the hard way. Now you can travel for days and not spot a single demon."

"What did Hell get in return?" Jason asked.

"The Sataners round up any humans they find and sacrifice their souls."

"The Sataners murder them?"

"Murder would be a blessing." Qiang paused. "Those to be sacrificed are slaughtered and their bodies used to make the monstrous humanoids that guard the gate."

Ustagov went pale. "Dear God."

Jason turned to the doctor. "What?"

"He's talking about the Golem."

"I'm not following you."

"Remember in my lab in Moscow? The Golem I autopsied? I told you that it had been constructed from hundreds of human body parts drawn together. Then we came across the decimation field outside of Changchun. The Sataners are butchering humans and transforming them into Golem."

"The Sataners are not doing the butchering," said Qiang. "That's being done by the vilest abomination to come through from the Underworld. We've been trying to track her down and kill her for months with no success."

"That's why we haven't come across anybody since we left Harbin," said Sook-kyoung.

"And why that town attacked us," added Sasha. "They must have thought we were Sataners."

Qiang shook his head with frustration. "Except for us and a few villages that stood their ground, everyone northeast of Beijing has either been rounded up by the Sataners or has fled. That's why we were leery of contacting you when you first arrived. We weren't sure if you were the ones we had heard about, wanderers, or followers coming to join the Sataners."

Father Belsario sat forward. "What do you mean 'the ones we had heard about'?"

"For months, rumors have spread across Asia about a group of adventurers who had closed a gate in west Europe.

We ignored them, dismissing them as stories people made up to bolster morale. Then we heard how those same adventurers closed gates in Moscow and Siberia. We started to feel optimistic, hoping there may be some truth to the rumors. Then you showed up in Harbin."

"Wait," interrupted Jason. "You've been watching us since Harbin?"

Qiang nodded.

"Why didn't you contact us?"

"We had to be certain you weren't a threat. After you were attacked by the residents of Shaoguodi and didn't seek revenge, we felt you could be trusted. Before we could make contact, you ran into the giant worms and got separated in the dust storm."

"They found me the morning after the storm ended," said Sook-kyoung. "They've treated me well since then. I trust them."

"We were about to reach out to the other members of your team. Before we could, they were taken in by the Sataners."

"Are they all right?" Jason blurted.

"They are, for now. They're at the Sataners camp not far from here."

"Why didn't you rescue them?'

"Because they willingly joined with the Sataners, which raised doubts. We wanted to contact you first to determine whether you were allies or a potential threat."

"How do you feel now?" Jason asked.

"That our two sides can work together."

"Then can we save our friends?"

"It's already in the works," Qiang reassured him. "We're going to sneak into their compound tonight, pull out your friends, and kill the Sataners. We wanted you there to make sure we didn't harm any of your people."

"Wait a minute," said Father Belsario. "You're planning on murdering the Sataners in their sleep."

"Yes." Qiang held up his hand to stop the cleric. "I know it seems cruel, but considering the suffering they've brought on others, it's actually a quite merciful—"

One of Qiang's horseman raced into the structure, panting for breath. A heated conversation took place in Mandarin. Qiang jumped up.

"There's been a change in plans. The Sataners moved out a few hours ago and are heading toward Doujiatun." Qiang turned to Jason. "And your friends are with them."

Jason stood up. "What does that mean?"

"It means if we don't reach them in time, they're dead."

CHAPTER TWENTY-EIGHT

MEI'S GROUP TRAVELED all morning and into the early afternoon. Jeanette wondered if they intended to break for lunch. She was about to go forward and talk to Mei when the column stopped. A moment later, a rider came back and paused by Jeanette.

"Mei want you... all you... to join her at front."

"Let's go."

The rider led them forward. Mei waited at the crest of a hill. At the base sat the village of Doujiatun. Its defenses were far inferior to the town she and Jason had come across a few days back. Other than being surrounded on three sides by a river and its estuary, this village had no defenses except for a guard tower near the entrance along the main road, and no one manned it.

Jeanette brought her horse alongside Mei. "Is this your stop?"

"Yes."

"What are we doing here? Will we be long?"

"We're here to sacrifice this town to the glory of Satan. You're here to bear witness to the splendid event."

Before the words fully sunk in, Jeanette heard weapons being cocked. Glancing over her shoulder, a dozen of Mei's people had formed a semi-circle around her and the others, aiming and ready to fire. Another dozen approached. Four grabbed the reins and steadied the animals. Four others pulled Ian and Vicky off their mounts, confiscated their AK-47s, and tied their hands behind their backs. Antoine fought back, kicking out with his right leg and smashing his boot into the face of the man attempting to take his Kalashnikov, breaking his jaw. The man dropped to his knees and cried. A set of hands grabbed Antoine from the left and pulled him out of his saddle. Once on the ground, the man hit Antoine on the head with the stock of his automatic rifle.

"Bai doesn't want him dead, she wants him subdued," warned Mei.

The beating stopped. The man yanked Antoine to his feet.

The last two approached Jeanette's horse. "Why are you doing this? We're no threat to you."

"You *are* a threat. You're here to shut the Gate to Salvation."

"You… you *want* to keep it open?"

"My dear, God walked away from China when China replaced Christianity with Communism. When the door opened, we had no divine grace to intervene on our behalf. There was nothing in this part of the world except dismay, death, and destruction. Bai changed all that. She agreed to recall those from the Underworld and bring peace to the region in exchange for our cooperation."

Jeanette sneered. "I'm afraid to ask what you do for her."

"There's nothing to be afraid of. Those who can't comprehend the significance of this event or refuse to join us are brought before Bai and sacrificed for the glory of Satan."

"You murder them?"

"We're not like those soulless, mindless creatures from the Underworld. We're human. Killing without purpose is a sin. What we do is for the benefit of humanity. Their deaths are required for a greater cause."

The nonchalant way in which Mei described mass slaughter terrified Jeanette. "What cause would that be?"

"That's what you're here to witness. I have to insist that you dismount and join your friends." Mei nodded, and the two soldiers moved in.

Jeanette thought about making a break for it but realized that, with a dozen mounted soldiers carrying Type 63s, she had little chance of getting away. Even if lucky enough to make it out, she would be leaving the others behind to certain death. She could not do that. Instead, she decided to comply and hopefully figure a way out later. Climbing down from her horse, Jeanette allowed herself to be disarmed and bound by the wrists.

Mei's people descended the hill. Most continued into the village. A dozen stayed on the outskirts, eight of them tending to the horses, the remaining four guarding Jeanette's group who were forced to kneel in the dirt and cross their ankles. They could only watch as events unfolded.

Commotion came from within the village, mostly yelling and crying, as the locals were removed from their homes. Most came along after being coaxed by Mei's people. Some had to be forced. The villagers were brought out in small groups and told to gather in a clearing. They complied, too scared to do anything else. Mothers hugged children. Elderly couples clasped hands, resigned to whatever fate awaited them. A few of the men talked quietly amongst themselves, their eyes scanning their captors. One teenage boy bolted from the crowd and headed for the road. He made it a hundred feet before two of Mei's guards caught up with him. The teenager resisted. Instead of shooting him, they broke his leg with the stocks of their Type 63s and dragged him back. The minor act of violence had the desired effect. The remaining villagers became compliant as more of their folk were rounded up. Jeanette wished she could do something to help, yet she was in no position to resist. Whatever happened to her team would hopefully be better than the fate that awaited the villagers.

THE DEMON HUNTERS and the *Xiongnu* had been traveling for

an hour when one of the horse-mounted scouts approached the column. Qiang ordered everyone to halt. A minute later, the scout rode up, and the two talked animatedly for several seconds. Qiang came over to Jason.

"The Sataners have already reached Doujiatun and are rounding up the villagers. We need to get there before the Seamstress if we hope to save them. Let's move."

Twenty minutes later, they stopped at the base of a hill half a mile from Doujiatun on the slope opposite the village. Qiang and two of his deputies climbed to the top. Jason, Haneef, Father Belsario, and Sasha joined them. They crouched and cautiously approached the crest. Below them, the Sataners had gathered the villagers into a cluster in the middle of a nearby field. Close to seventy-five soldiers stood in a circle around them.

Qiang leaned over, nudged Jason, and pointed to the area around the horses. "There are your people."

Jason's heart jumped at the sight of Jeanette. His anger seethed when he saw her bound by the wrists and surrounded by armed guards. "Are you going to rescue the villagers?"

"Yes."

"We'll help. We can save our people and take out the Sataners guarding the horses."

"Good. Just keep Mei alive. She needs to be dealt with—"

One of the deputies interrupted Qiang and pointed west. Three horses approached the camp, one in front and two slightly to the rear and on either side.

"We're too late," said Qiang. "The Seamstress is here."

"It's not over," argued Jason. "We have the same numbers as they do, plus we have the element of surprise."

"Not against the Seamstress." Qiang began to climb down the slope. "We should get going before they find us, or we'll be dead, too."

Jason grabbed Qiang's arm. "I need to see this."

"You really don't."

"Go if you want." Jason released Qiang's arm. "We're staying."

Qiang sighed and lay down on the crest beside Jason. "You'll regret this."

CHAPTER TWENTY-NINE

"**T**HIS LOOKS LIKE trouble," Antoine whispered to Jeanette. "What does?"

"That." He motioned with his head toward the west.

Three horses approached, one in front and two slightly behind on either side. The figures riding the rearmost horses wore black cloaks that covered their heads and hands and extended below the stirrups. The rider of the lead horse wore a similar cloak, only crimson in color. All three leaned forward in their saddles so that the cloaks draped over their faces. Even the horses lowered their heads, their gait slow and menacing. The animals stopped fifty feet from the villagers. Their riders did not move.

"This is Bai." Mei's voice tingled with excitement. Before Jeanette could respond, Mei rushed over to greet the riders. When she reached the lead, she dropped to her knees and bowed her head.

"It's pleasurable to see you again," said a female voice from under the cowl, the voice unnerving yet somehow sensuous at the same time.

"The pleasure is mine, my Mistress." Mei rose to her feet and held out her left hand. The cloaked figure took it and slid out of the saddle. The other two figures did the same, standing by their horses with their heads lowered.

"They're waiting for you, my Mistress." Mei gestured to the villagers. Bai strolled toward them, her movement undiscernible beneath the folds, giving her motion a spectral appearance. She stopped several yards from the villagers, oblivious to the panic her presence caused. After a few seconds, the cloaked head nodded.

"As always, my child, you've done well. I am satisfied."

Mei's expression beamed, and her body stiffened with pride. "Thank you, my Mistress."

"Proceed."

Mei approached the villagers and extended her arms in greeting. "Brothers and sisters, allow me to introduce you to Bai. She is about to bestow upon you the greatest gift that can be offered—the gift of salvation."

"What if we don't want to be saved?" yelled an elderly man from amongst the villagers.

Mei began to respond when Bai interrupted. Her rough voice took on a tone that was soft and reassuring, unsettling yet mesmerizing. "Then consider it the gift of freedom."

"Freedom from what?"

"Freedom from fear. Freedom from uncertainty. Freedom from eternal damnation."

Bai reached up and pulled the cloak back over her body and down her shoulders, allowing it to fall to the ground. Mei rushed forward to pick up the garment. A gasp shot through the villagers. Despite all the horrors Jeanette had seen these past months, even she was shocked by the sight.

Bai had been stitched together from various human body parts, giving her a Frankenstein-like appearance; yet somehow, she remained enticingly beautiful. Long brunette hair cascaded down her back. A scar ran from her hairline, down the center of her forehead, veered right of her nose and mouth, and then cut back to the center of her chin and down her neck. The skin to the right was Caucasian, that to the left Mediterranean. One eye was azure blue and the other dark green. Another scar ran around the circumference of her neck, the skin below Asian in tone. A bikini-sized leather bra covered her breasts, not enough to conceal the fact that each possessed a different shape and size. A third scar circled Bai's left arm just above the shoulder, with the arm below it tanned and feminine. A fourth scar appeared just below her right shoulder, the arm beneath longer by a few inches and more masculine, with a light African coloration. Bai wore leather pants and knee-high boots. Jeanette felt certain that if Bai's legs were visible, they would be as patchwork as the rest of her body. Bai spread her arms wide.

"When you give yourselves unto My Lord Satan and me, we are granting you freedom from the uselessness of your mortal existence to serve a much greater cause."

"We will never serve you or Satan willingly," yelled the elderly man.

"Your willingness is not necessary for your servitude."

Bai snapped her fingers. Her two companions surged forward. They stopped beside Bai and shed their cloaks. Panic spread through the villagers. The creatures were humanoid in shape, only slimmer and taller than any man. They had no distinctive features other than blood red eyes that glowed sunk deep into their skulls. The creatures were more shadow than corporeal, and their bodies flickered like the image on a television with bad reception. When they stood erect to their full height of seven feet, the demons raised their hands in front of them. They were elongated, with palms almost a foot in length and a pair of pointed, thumb-like appendages jutting out from the base. Three sets of fingers on each hand, each six inches long, curled and uncurled. The fingers ended in eight-inch talons shaped like curved knives, each glistening in the sunlight.

Bai lifted her masculine arm and held it with the palm out perpendicular to the ground. "It's time, my lovelies."

Slits appeared along the lower faces of the demons, forming into mouths filled with rows of fangs of various sizes.

The next few moments played out in such a frenzy Jeanette barely registered them. The demons crouched and hissed, an unearthly sound that emanated from deep in their throats, sending a wave of terror through the villagers. Some cried or screamed; others dropped to their knees, too scared to react. A few attempted to run. Bai stiffened her outstretched hand. Ice blue light flowed from her palm and washed over the villagers, freezing them in mid-stance. A moment later, the twin demons lunged. They moved so rapidly Jeanette could not distinguish their actions. She focused on a young woman clutching her seven-year-old child. A demon raced up, its motions highly accelerated and blurred, momentarily blocking the two from view. When it moved on to its next victim, the mother and child had been sliced apart. Blood flowed from hundreds of slashes. All the villagers suffered the same fate, soaking the grass red. When the demons finished their massacre they retreated, taking up position on either side of Bai. Gore stained their bodies and dripped from their talons, pooling in a crimson puddle beneath them.

Bai lowered her arm, extinguishing the ice blue light. At that point, the bodies of the villagers, no longer frozen in place, fell to pieces. The severed portions of limbs and organs slid to the ground, creating huge piles of human detritus onto which their skeletons collapsed. They had not been slaughtered so much as methodically and precisely dissected, with muscles and flesh sliced from the bones as if they were cuts of meat and organs eviscerated completely intact. The butchery had ended almost as soon as it had begun.

Four of the Sataners stepped forward, picked up the discarded cloaks, and draped them back over the demons. Within seconds, the material became soaked with blood.

Only then did Jeanette realize that Vicky knelt beside her, sobbing uncontrollably. Tears and snot flowed down her cheeks as she snorted back phlegm. Ian bent over and retched. Antoine stood to Jeanette's left, his expression stoic, fury burning in his eyes. Jeanette stood in front of Mei.

"You've made your point. You're in charge."

"You don't understand." Mei met her gaze. Her tone was not sarcastic or cruel, but filled with love and adoration, which made it even more menacing. "This is not to make a point. This is the first stage in Satan's miracle."

JASON AND THE others watched as the Sataners rounded up the villagers. When Mei summoned the three cloaked figures, Jason closed his eyes and attempted to sense their aura. Although he picked up nothing from the one in front, he detected malevolence from the two in the rear, greater and darker than anything he had experienced before, which meant they were most likely demons. He felt something familiar emanating off them, what could best be described as a lingering imprint of tormented, like those of the Golem. Switching his attention to the figure cloaked in crimson, this time he sensed a soul, but not a human one, or, more precisely, not a modern one. This soul was ancient.

"My God," mumbled Sasha when the Seamstress disrobed. "She's hideous."

"That's nothing." Qiang pointed to the two cloaked figures behind her. "Those are the demons the Seamstress uses to help create her monstrosities. We call them decimators."

"Why do you call them that?" Haneef asked.

"You're about to find out."

The decimators shed their cloaks and tore into the villagers. Jason's sixth sense spiked, overriding his emotions. He felt the anguish of every soul being butchered, their agony and terror. Each death intensified the sensation until Jason feared he would go insane. He shoved his right wrist into his mouth and bit, stifling the scream that roared inside of him. When a pair of hands clasped his shoulders, he lashed out, fearing a decimator had latched onto him. It took several moments to realize it was Sasha comforting him.

"We have to get him out of here now," she said to Qiang.

"No." Jason forced himself to sit up. His body shivered and sweat covered his forehead and back, drenching his flightsuit and winter coat. He struggled to tamp down the tormented auras and regain control of his thoughts and emotions, barely able to do either. Only after the villagers were dead was he able to manage the sensations. "It's okay. The worst is over."

Qiang shook his head. "You have no idea how wrong you are."

BAI STEPPED TOWARD the scene of the massacre, stopping fifteen feet away. She extended her feminine arm toward the decimation field, the palm down and the fingers spread wide. With a flick of the wrist, she spun the palm upward. The villagers' remains pulsated. Bai manipulated her fingers and twitched her hand. Muscles and skin slid along the ground toward the center of the field, merging. As one set of muscles attached to another, the seam between them melded and joined with the next, until the legs of all the slaughtered villagers had formed a pair of Golem legs. One by one, each set of organs was pulled from the field and coalesced to create a single, larger version belonging to the creature. Over one hundred human stomachs, kidneys, livers, intestines, and more blended into their monstrous demonic counterparts. As the hearts combined, each began beating until they did so in unison. When the internal organs were in place, layers of skin and muscles slid up the legs and wrapped around the body cavity, creating a protective covering. The arms came together in the same manner, followed by the head. Human brains cascaded up the body and gathered around the top of the head. With each pulsation of the mass, the brains melded together and became one. Skin and muscles stretched over the upper torso and shoulders, shaping the creature's bulbous head. The eyes developed last, hundreds of human pairs melting and mixing into twin milky orbs. When finished, the monstrosity stood over thirty feet tall with a massive torso, thick and muscular legs, bulky arms as long as the demon's body, and dark red skin. Bai brought her hand in front of her face and shoved it forward, palm facing the Golem. A bolt of whitish-yellow light shot out, engulfing the demon. The body crackled and smoked. Finally, the eyes opened and a spark of life glowed in them. The Golem stretched its limbs and twisted its neck from side to side. A moment later, it stood erect and lumbered over to Bai. She issued a command in an ancient language. The Golem turned south and shambled toward Shenyang.

Bai hunched forward from exhaustion. Mei went to her assistance. Bai waved her off. It took several seconds for her to recover enough strength to stand and stroll over to Jeanette.

"What do you think of my talents?" Bai asked.

"You're even more monstrous than that thing you created."

Mei seethed and stepped forward, raising her hand to strike Jeanette. Bai warned off her minion. When Mei backed down, Bai focused her attention on Jeanette.

"I'm sorry you feel that way. It'll make things that much worse for you."

"Why do you say that?"

"Because you and your friends are going to become part of a Golem once we've reached the Gate to Salvation."

CHAPTER THIRTY

BACK AT THE factory, Jason rested inside the corrugated steel building on a stack of pillows piled in one corner. Sasha lie beside him, stroking his forehead. Lucifer was on the other side, using Jason's leg as a pillow; every few minutes the werehound would lift his head to check on him. Lilith sat on her haunches at his feet, her head raised, and her eyes locked on her master.

When the Seamstress had pulled together the villagers' body parts into a Golem, Jason's sixth sense spiked. The anguish from the tormented souls being spliced into that monstrosity overwhelmed him. He felt the individual suffering of each victim and could not handle it. As much as Jason tried to block them, every second of the Golem's transformation drained him of his physical and emotional endurance, and his other senses shut down. He had a vague memory of indistinguishable and panicked voices around him, followed by hands grasping him, helping him to stand, and lifting him onto his horse. Only after several minutes had passed and the group had retreated far enough from the decimation field did the overpowering feeling of suffering subside. Even then, his other senses remained clouded. Sasha had ridden beside him the entire way back to the factory, keeping him propped up in his saddle, and she and Father Belsario had carried him from the horse into the building. Jason only remembered snippets of the trip. Everything gradually returned to normal after he had been able to sleep for a while. Now he relaed on the pillows, listening to the others around the fire in the middle of the building discuss what had happened earlier.

Haneef stared into the bottom of his cup of tea. "I can't believe what we saw today."

"Believe it," said Qiang. The matter-of-fact tone to his voice sounded chilling under the circumstances. "That's been going on for months."

"Why haven't you stopped them?" Matthew asked.

"We tried once, about two months ago. One of our larger patrols came across the Seamstress about to perform the ritual and attacked. Our people were slaughtered. Only one of twenty-eight horsemen survived. The decimators ripped them apart in seconds."

"Maybe you can't kill the demons," said Vicky. "Why not get rid of the Sataners?"

"We do. Every time we kill one, Mei builds their ranks with more followers. Even the leaders are replaceable. We've taken out two of them already, and someone else always steps forward to fill the position. Mei is the third person we know of to lead the cult." Qiang drank from his cup. "All we're able to do is whittle away at the Sataners. We're too outnumbered to take on the Seamstress or the decimators."

"Your best bet is to shut down the portal," said Ustagov.

"Why is that?"

"Every demon that passes through into our realm is somehow connected to it. When you close the portal, the demons perish."

"All of them? Including the Seamstress and the decimators?"

Ustagov nodded.

"Then the rumors are true. You've found a way of closing them?"

"We have."

"How is that possible?"

"The portals were created because of an experiment with antimatter. One of our group, who is no longer with us, created an antimatter device that will destroy the portal. All we have to do is get close enough to throw it in. That's why we're here."

"That's excellent." Qiang's excitement was palpable. "It's only a few days ride by horse. If we leave tomorrow morning, we can end all of this within a week. I'll have my people get everything ready—"

"Not so fast," interrupted Haneef. "First, we have to rescue our friends from the Sataners. We need them to help close the portal."

"Qiang's right," said Jason. He opened his eyes and sat up on the pillows, even that minimal effort draining his energy. "We need to close that portal before we do anything else."

"What about the others?" asked Sook-kyoung. "They're still alive. They won't be for long unless we rescue them."

"There's nothing we can do can keep them alive." Jason crawled to his knees and attempted to stand. His legs gave way from under him. Sasha wrapped her arm around his back and under his left arm, propping him up. It took a moment for him to get his footing. When he felt strong enough to walk, he patted Sasha's hand. She released Jason but stayed beside him. "You heard Qiang. They've already tried to stop the Seamstress and decimators and lost twenty-seven men in the process. We can't afford such losses. Besides, she doesn't plan on killing the others yet."

"Why do you say that?" asked Gabriel.

"She would have done it when she created the Golem and would have included them in its formation." Jason staggered over to the team, swaying slightly. "She knows who they are and is saving them for something much more sinister."

"You mean like a special ritual?" asked Matthew.

Father Belsario's eyes widened. "Or an offering."

"Exactly. What better way to please Satan than to sacrifice Demon Hunters at his door. Our best chance of saving them is get to the portal first and close it." Jason turned to Qiang, "You said it's a few days' journey from here?"

"Two days, to be exact. If we leave tomorrow morning, we should arrive there early to late evening the next day."

"Good," said Jason. "Then we leave at midnight and double time it. I want to get there the morning of the second day so we don't have to battle the Demon Spawn in the dark."

"It's dangerous to travel at night," warned Qiang.

"It's even more dangerous to let Mei and the Seamstress get there before us. I understand your concerns. If you don't want to go, just give us the directions and we'll do this by ourselves."

The expression on Qiang's face showed both anger and embarrassment. Jason's tone became more conciliatory. "You've lost too many good people already. No one here will think any less of you if you don't want to go."

Qiang appreciated the gesture that allowed him to save face. He stood and bowed. "My people will accompany you."

"Are you sure?"

"You've come halfway around the world to close the Gate to Salvation. I owe it to my ancestors and China's future to give you all the help we can."

Jason bowed to Qiang. When he did, his knees wobbled. Sasha reached out to him, but he waved her off. Taking a deep breath, Jason stood upright. "Thank you."

"I'll have my people get everything ready to leave at midnight. Let me know what you need and we'll take care of you."

"Father Belsario and Haneef will work with you. I'd send out a few scouts to follow the Sataners and report their progress back to us. We need to make sure we beat them to the portal if we're going to be successful."

"I'll get on that right away."

Jason bowed again, only this time being careful not to disrupt his balance. Qiang rushed out to prepare for their departure, followed by Jason's team. Only Sasha and the werehounds remained behind. When the others had left, Sasha took Jason by the hand and led him back toward the pillows.

"Come on. You need to rest."

"I'm fine," Jason protested, although he did not let go of her hand.

"No, you're not. You can barely stand. And I didn't come back to Earth to babysit you." When he tried to respond, Sasha placed the middle and index fingers of her free hand against his lips. They felt warm and soft. She led him back and stood over Jason as he settled into the pillows. Lucifer and Lilith settled in on each side of their master and snuggled.

"Thanks, Sasha."

"You know I'd do anything for you. Now get some rest." Sasha went to leave and paused. "You realize how much danger you're putting the others in by not rescuing them and closing the portal instead?"

"Are you asking this because you're concerned I might not be thinking clearly after today's trauma?"

"I'm wondering why you're putting Jeanette at such a risk."

"She's in just as much danger as the rest of us, and she knew that when she asked to come along."

"But you... you..."

"Care for her?"

Sasha lowered her head.

"My feelings for Jeanette are irrelevant. It's the same as in Paris when I let you lead the Demon Spawn away from the portal inside Notre Dame. I knew I would never see you again, and it broke my heart."

Sasha's head shot up. "Did it really?"

"Of course. I love you. I've lost everybody I love because of this damn apocalypse. My mother and father. Doc. You. I'm going to continue to lose people I care about as long as these portals exist."

"We've all lost people we care about."

"I can empathize." Jason spoke the words without emotion. "The difference is you've watched our friends die, while I'm the one who made the decisions that sent them to their deaths. I know what we're doing is noble, and we all volunteered for this. Every time one of us is killed, I tell myself their sacrifice will save the hundreds of thousands of people struggling to survive, if there are even that many left. I tell myself that everything that happened in Paris, Moscow, and Lake Baikal is for the greater good, and in the end more lives will be saved because of the sacrifices we're making. Rationally I can accept that. Emotionally I can't. Every time one of us dies a piece of my soul dies with them."

Sasha knelt beside Jason and placed her hand on his leg. "You can't allow this to consume you. I ne… we need you."

"I'm not letting it consume me. I tamp down my feelings."

"Don't do that. One of the things that makes you so special, and that makes you a good leader, is your emotions."

"I can't lead my friends to their death and still maintain my emotions if I want to keep my sanity." Jason drooped his head, a sad expression that betrayed the conflict raging within him. "I don't know what bothers me more: the fact that I made the decision to abandon Jeanette and the others to a horrific death, or the callousness with which I made it."

Sasha struggled to hold back her tears.

Jason clasped her hand. She squeezed it, her touch tender. It felt good. Jason was pleased he still had some emotions left.

"Thanks for being here. If you don't mind, I'm exhausted and need to rest. Wake me around eleven."

Without waiting for an answer, Jason laid back into the pillows. He fell asleep immediately and did not hear Sasha sobbing as she exited the building.

CHAPTER THIRTY-ONE

THE DAY HAD been exceptionally arduous for Jeanette. First, they had to witness the butchering of the villagers and the creation of the Golem from the body parts. Then Mei took her and the Demon Hunters prisoner, confiscating their horses so they could not attempt an escape and forcing them to travel on foot. Each had their hands bound in front of them, with one end of the rope attached to the saddle of a Sataner's horse. Jeanette estimated they had traveled five or six miles with no breaks and no water. She began to get thirsty two hours into their trek; by the time the Sataners stopped for the night, she could barely swallow due to the dryness in her throat. As Mei's people erected tents, a young Chinese woman barely out of her teen years came over and offered Antoine a canteen of water. He took it without offering any thanks, swigged a mouthful, and passed it to his friends.

Several minutes elapsed before Mei and five of her followers approached, four of the latter with their Type 63 automatic rifles drawn and ready to fire. The fifth untied the rope from each of the saddles, clutching the ends in her right hand. Jeanette fought back the urge to wrap the length of rope around the woman's neck and strangle her.

"What's going to happen to us?" she asked Mei.

"We're preparing a tent for you to sleep." Mei spoke the words with the pleasantness of a hotel clerk welcoming a guest. "You need to rest. We have a long day ahead of us tomorrow."

"Where are you taking us?" Ian asked.

"To the Gate to Salvation. Bai will meet us there."

"What will happen once we get there?"

"You will all be part of a glorious ritual that will free you from your misery." Mei walked off. "Bring them this way."

The young woman followed. As the ropes grew taut, Jeanette and the others refused to move. One of the guards stepped forward and shoved Jeanette in the back with his weapon. Antoine moved toward him, his fist clenched. Jeanette shook her head and started walking. The others fell in beside her.

Mei led them to a tent in the center of the compound and pulled aside the flap. Inside, a sixth guard waited. He held four sets of shackles connected to each other by a thick chain. As the Demon Hunters entered, he attached one set to each ankle and locked them in place. When all four had been secured, the young woman untied the ropes.

Jeanette motioned toward the shackles. "What are these for?"

"To prevent you from escaping, of course." Mei turned to one of her guards. "If you do try to get away, my people have orders to shoot you in the leg, which will make it difficult for you to travel. So, please, for your own sake, don't try anything foolish."

The young woman exited the tent accompanied by the gunmen. Mei stopped before letting the flap close and said, "You should get some sleep. I'll have someone bring you dinner once it's cooked."

After everyone had departed, Antoine lowered himself onto the dirt and immediately fell asleep. Vicky sat down and crossed her legs. Tears ran down her cheeks.

Jeanette knelt beside her and wrapped her left arm around Vicky's shoulders. "Everything will be all right."

Vicky brushed her arm away. "No, it won't. We're going to die, just like those villagers."

"Jason will rescue us."

Vicky snorted derisively. "He left us after the dust storm to close that damn portal. Face it, we're on our own, and we're going to die."

Jeanette reached out a hand to comfort her. Vicky slapped it aside. She collapsed and curled into a fetal position as she cried.

Ian crouched beside Jeanette. "Leave her alone. A good cry and some rest are the best things for her right now."

Jeanette moved as far away from Vicky as the chain allowed and sat. Ian lay down nearby and locked his hands behind his head into a makeshift pillow. A few moments of awkward silence passed before she asked, "Do you think Jason and the rest of the team survived the dust storm?"

"I'm sure some of them made it through alive. We did."

"Then why hasn't Jason rescued us?"

Ian hesitated. "He's probably still trying to find us. It's been several days since we were separated."

"You don't believe that. You agree with Vicky that he left us behind to close the portal."

Ian lowered his voice to a whisper. "I wouldn't blame him if he did."

"How can you say that?"

"Because the smart thing to do is close the portal as quickly as possible, remove the demon threat to the area, and then come for us."

"That doesn't bother you?"

"That's what I would do." Ian closed his eyes and settled on the dirt. "If I were you, I'd get some rest while you can. We're going to be doing a lot of walking tomorrow."

Ian dozed off within a few minutes. Vicky cried herself to sleep not long after. Jeanette sat there, staring at the walls of the tent for a while before settling down herself. Although rationally she knew Jason had to proceed with their quest, it upset her that he had not bothered to search for them. She would have made the effort because she loved him. Maybe that was the problem—she cared for Jason far more than he did for her. For the first time since leaving Mont St. Michel, she felt as though she had come along for all the wrong reasons or should not have come along at all.

As exhaustion overwhelmed Jeanette and she fell asleep, she had one final thought. Part of her felt certain that if Sasha had been the one separated from the rest of the group, Jason would have made every possible effort to find her.

CHAPTER THIRTY-TWO

JASON WOKE UP an hour before midnight. Except for still being a little drained from the afternoon's events and slightly disoriented from sleeping so late, he felt better than when he had arrived back at the factory. Rolling to one side, he expected to bump into Lucifer or Lilith snuggled against him. The werehounds were not there. He rested for a few moments before gathering his gear. As he did, the door opened and Sasha entered, with Lucifer and Lilith right behind her.

"Oh, good. You're up." Sasha sauntered over to him. The werehounds raced ahead, tails wagging, to greet their master. "I came by to wake you."

"I've been up for a while." Jason scratched Lucifer and Lilith behind the ears. The latter licked his face.

"How do you feel?"

"Much better." Jason stood. "Are we almost ready?"

"We're waiting on you. Are you sure you're up to it?"

"No problem." Jason took a step forward and stumbled. Sasha reached out for him. He clasped her hand and shook his head. Sasha wrapped her fingers around his and squeezed affectionately before releasing her grip. The two of them stepped outside and Sasha led him to the compound's gate.

The Demon Hunters and their horses had gathered by the exterior wall. Scores of *Xiongnu* horsemen huddled nearby. Qiang stood to one side talking with three women in their early twenties. When finished, the women bowed deeply at the waist, mounted their horses, and rode off. Qiang waved Jason over. Sasha led the werehounds to the rest of his team.

Qiang nodded as Jason approached. "I trust you're feeling better."

"I am." Jason gestured toward the *Xiongnu* horsemen. "Are they going with us?"

"Yes. These are all my mounted archers. There are sixty-nine of us, including myself. We're going to escort you to the gate and help you close it."

"Isn't it dangerous leaving your compound without protection?"

"As you said the other day, our best chance of survival is to stop the demons from entering this realm. The quicker we do that, the safer we all are. It's a calculated risk leaving my people undefended for two days, but it's one I'm willing to take."

"And what happens if we fail and your archers are killed?"

Qiang shrugged. "In that case, it will only be a matter of time before we're all dead anyway."

Jason could not argue with Qiang's logic. He pointed in the direction the three young women had ridden off. "What are they doing?"

"They're going to follow the Sataners and report back to me on their progress."

"Are you anticipating trouble?"

Qiang shook his head. "We should have more than enough time to get to the gate before the Sataners. If there's any change, I want to know about it before it surprises us."

"Good thinking."

"Are you ready to head out?"

Jason glanced at those around him. Their force contained his own team of four, four Purgatoriati, and sixty-nine *Xiongnu* horsemen, which should be more than enough to clear a path to the portal long enough for him to deploy the antimatter device.

"Let's head out."

Qiang issued an order in Mandarin to his archers, who all bowed and mounted their horses. Jason's people did the same.

Qiang led the way through the mounds of debris surrounding the factory and headed for the nearest road. Once there, he led his horse south toward Shenyang, with the others close behind. Lucifer and Lilith stayed close to Jason. The lights from the campfires at the factory were soon engulfed by the night, and the group made its way through the dark toward their destination.

CHAPTER THIRTY-THREE

A COMMOTION OUTSIDE their tent roused Jeanette from her sleep. At first, she thought Mei's people were preparing to sacrifice them to Bai in another Golem-making ritual. Then she smelled the aroma of food being cooked and realized it must be time for breakfast. Jeanette woke the others. It took two attempts with Antoine. A few minutes later, Mei and four of her followers entered. One brandished a Type 63 automatic rifle, which he held in front of him, ready to use if necessary. The other three carried breakfast. The youngest, a boy no older than ten, handed each of the Demon Hunters a small plastic bowl and a cup, and then the other two served white rice and water.

"Good morning," said Mei with a cheery tone. "I hope you all slept well."

Jeanette forewent any platitudes. She stared at the rice and water. "Is this what we're getting for breakfast? Prison rations?"

"You're getting the same food and portions the rest of us do. We treat you no different."

Ian snorted. "You'd think Satan's mates would be given better food than this."

"Eating to excess is one of the many sins mankind developed when we abandoned religion for Communism." Mei sounded befuddled, not angry. "We consume what we need to stay alive and strong. We chose rice and water because they were the staples of our ancestors. Now please, eat. You need to keep your strength up. We have a long day ahead of us."

The servers left the tent, followed by Mei and the gunman.

Ian sat down, crossed his legs, and shoveled rice into his mouth with his fingers.

"What are you doing?" asked Jeanette.

"Mei may be crazy, but she's right about keeping up our strength."

Jeanette hesitated. She hated the idea of doing what Mei requested. She also knew that they needed to be ready to fight back if the opportunity presented itself. Giving in to the inevitable, Jeanette sat and ate.

After a few minutes, Jeanette asked Antoine, "How are you doing?"

"I'm fine." The Moroccan stared at her quizzically. "Why do you ask?"

"You collapsed last night when we got into the tent and slept straight through until morning."

"I'm exhausted. I've been riding the horse so long I'm not used to walking."

"Good. I thought we were losing you."

Antoine chuckled. "You don't have to worry about me. When the time comes, I'll be ready to bust heads."

Vicky stared at her bowl of rice and mumbled something Jeanette did not hear. "I didn't get that."

"I know I'm the one you're really worried about." Vicky lifted her head. "I freaked out on you last night. I'm sorry."

"There's no need to apologize," Jeanette reassured her. "It happens to everyone."

"No, it doesn't. You and Antoine have gone through much more than me and are still holding it together. And Ian is enjoying this."

Ian was taken aback. "I wouldn't say I'm enjoying this. I expected it to be dangerous and exciting. It's one of the reasons I asked to join."

Vicky lowered her head again so she could cry. "I'm here for the wrong reason."

"What do you mean?" Ian asked.

Jeanette interrupted, wanting to save Vicky the need to explain why she had to leave the predatory situation at Mont St. Michel. "You have to believe me when I say it's all right. You've done nothing you need to be ashamed or embarrassed about."

Vicky raised her head. "I promise I won't let you down again."

"You haven't," Jeanette reassured her. "I'm the one who let you down."

Vicky sniffed back her tears. "How?"

Jeanette sighed. "Antoine tried to warn me not to trust Mei and I didn't listen to him. I thought I knew better. I wanted to prove I'm as capable of leading as Jason and... and...."

Vicky tried to comfort her. "It's okay."

"It's not! I screwed up and we're probably going to die." Jeanette faced Antoine. "I'm sorry I ignored your advice."

The Moroccan nodded. "Don't worry about it."

"How can I not? If I had listened to you rather than being so arrogant, none of us would be in this situation."

"We've been in worse."

"Not because of bad decisions."

"None of us blame you for this," said Vicky, trying to comfort her friend.

"I don't," added Antoine.

Jeanette stared at Ian, who for a moment said nothing. He finally realized that she expected a response. "I probably would have done the same thing you did."

"Thank you." Jeanette forced a smile. "I—"

The sound of approaching footsteps forced an end to the conversation. Five of Mei's people entered, four of them holding Type 63s. They stood in each corner as the fifth went from prisoner to prisoner, unfastening the shackles. When finished, he gestured for them to follow. At first, Jeanette refused to move until one of the guards stepped forward and raised his weapon. They exited the tent. Eight more of Mei's people greeted them outside. As four of them broke down the tent, the rest tied the Demon Hunters' wrists together with rope and attached the loose end to the saddle of a horse.

Ten minutes later, the camp set out on the road to Shenyang.

★ ★ ★

FROM THE COPSE of trees on a small hillock half a mile away, Xiu lay prone and watched the Sataners through a pair of binoculars. "Where are the outsiders?"

"Keep looking," ordered her sister, Lihua, who lay on the grass beside her. She also scanned the compound through a pair of binoculars. "They have to be down there somewhere."

"Unless Mei killed them already."

"God forbid." Lihua spun her head toward her sister. Her brunette ponytail slapped against her cheek. "Don't joke about things like that."

"I'm not joking."

"Knock that off. We promised Qiang—"

Off to Lihua's left, Zhen whispered, "I found them."

"Where?" Lihua asked.

Zhen lowered her binoculars and pointed. "In the center of the compound where the Sataners are taking down the tent. The outsiders are being tied to four horses."

Xiu focused on that location. "I see them."

"Are they okay?" asked Lihua. She still scanned the compound, unable to find them.

"As well as can be expected."

Lihua found the outsiders, two men and two women, standing behind the horses they were lashed to.

The three women watched for close to an hour as the Sataners finished breaking down camp and then set out for the gate. Xiu watched the direction the Sataners went until they disappeared over the horizon and calculated their direction on the map. Once certain the caravan had traveled out of sight, she stood, removed a notepad and pen from her jacket pocket, and jotted a message. Ripping off the top sheet, Xiu folded it and handed it to Zhen.

"Take this to Qiang. Let him know the Sataners are traveling south through the countryside between the G1 and the G25, and don't appear to be in any hurry."

"Yes, ma'am." Zhen took the paper and slid it into her trouser pocket. "What about you?"

"Lihua and I will follow the Sataners. If there is any change in their movement, I'll send her to Qiang with the details. Join us as soon as you can."

"How will I find you?"

Xiu considered it for a moment. "Do you have your compass with you?"

Zhen removed it from her pocket, flipped open the top, and aligned the arrow with north.

"Good," said Xiu. "Note where the Sataners are heading. After you talk to Qiang, come back here and follow us. I have chalk. We'll leave marks. An X means they're staying on course, an arrow indicates if they change direction. Understood?"

Zhen nodded. Mounting her horse, she rode off as fast as possible toward the factory. When the woman had left, Lihua asked her sister, "Now what?"

"We track the Sataners until Qiang and the outsiders close the gate."

CHAPTER THIRTY-FOUR

T HE DEMON HUNTERS and the *Xiongnu* had been traveling along the G1 all night and well into the morning with only a few brief breaks. By sunrise, they had reached the northern outskirts of Kaiyuan. A few hours later, they had bypassed the town and were heading toward Yinzhou. To ensure nothing snuck up on them, either human or demon, Qiang had stationed four five-man patrols one mile ahead and behind the main group as well as on either flank. Because of these early warning pickets, they had been able to move faster than normal.

Ustagov brought his horse alongside of Jason's and kept pace. "Do you mind if we talk?"

"Sure."

"I'm concerned about how you reacted the other day to the killing of the villagers and the formation of the Golem."

"I'm fine. Just overwhelmed by so many souls being slaughtered at once."

"I know you're fine physically." Ustagov shook his head. "I've been analyzing how you reacted, and I think there may be a way for you to better control your sixth sense."

"Why do you think that?"

"You told me earlier you can sense beings that once had souls, like the flesh eaters, or were made from people with souls, like the ravagers and Golem. And you can detect the auras of certain people you're emotionally close to, such as Sasha."

"That's right."

SCOTT M. BAKER

Ustagov gestured toward the werehounds. "You also pick up the auras of Lilith and Lucifer, yet they don't possess souls."

Jason contemplated what the doctor had said. "You know, I hadn't thought about that."

"I hadn't either until I witnessed your reaction at the decimation field."

"What do you think it means?"

"It means you possess the ability to pick up the aura emitted by anything, human or demonic," Ustagov answered. "You haven't fully developed the skill yet. So far, you've only sensed auras that are very intense or that have strong feelings of affection toward you. You've always thought that was the extent of your ability. It's not. It's the baseline."

Jason had no idea what Ustagov meant. "Now you've lost me."

"Your sixth sense can easily pick up extremes. By contrast, you should also have the ability to detect auras that are subtle."

Jason had never considered it before. What Ustagov proposed made perfect sense. If he could perfect that skill, then in the future he could avoid incidents like what occurred when the giant insects ambushed his team in the Paris Metro. "How do I perfect it?"

"Since you know it can be done, practice on detecting our auras. Once you've honed your sixth sense, picking up those of other humans or Demon Spawn will be easy."

"Do you really think it'll work?"

"I don't know why it wouldn't. It makes—"

Ustagov's words trailed off, his attention drawn to the front of the column. Two of the *Xiongnu* horsemen guarding their southern flank approached, escorting a third horse. Jason recognized the latter's rider as one of the young women Qiang had been talking to the night before. When they reached him, the two guards headed back to their station. Qiang chatted with the young woman for a moment, and then the two rode over to Jason.

"We have good news," said Qiang. "Your missing team members are still alive. The Sataners are twelve kilometers to our south and several kilometers behind us. They're making their way toward the gate and are in no hurry. We should get there and have plenty of time to close it before they arrive."

Jason allowed himself a slight grin. It was the first good news he had received in a long time.

Qiang said to Zhen, "Head back with the others and keep us apprised of any change in the situation."

"I will."

"Good job out there."

Zhen bowed. She spurred her horse and headed back.

"I'm going to order everyone to stand down for a few hours," said Qiang.

Jason shook his head. "We know we have the advantage. Let's exploit it."

"We've been marching for ten hours. The horses are exhausted and can't go on. We need to give them a break or they'll be no use to us when we reach the gate."

Jason tried to protest when Ustagov cut him off. "Qiang's right. The Sataners are nowhere near the portal. We need to be rested if we hope to close it."

Jason gave in to the inevitable. "Sorry. I want to get this over with."

"No need to apologize," said Qiang. "We're not that far away. If we rest for six hours, we should reach the gate early tomorrow morning."

CHAPTER THIRTY-FIVE

JEANETTE DID NOT know what bothered her more—having to walk all day with her hands lashed to a horse's saddle or having to trudge through all the shit the animals left in their wake. By late morning, Jeanette felt filthy and exhausted. She was relieved when Mei's people stopped for lunch. That feeling was short-lived, however, when Mei refused to untie them. The Demon Hunters had to stand or kneel by the horses and struggle to drink from a single canteen of water that they passed between them.

Ian took a long gulp and handed the canteen to Vicky. Because her hands were tied, she had difficulty grasping it. The canteen slipped and almost dropped into a steaming pile of fresh horse dung. Ian caught it at the last moment.

"Thanks," Vicky said sheepishly. She drank so quickly some of the water spilled out of her mouth and ran down her chin. "I wonder how much longer we'll have to travel like this."

"It shouldn't be too long," Ian answered. "By my estimates, we're probably thirty to forty miles from Shenyang, and even closer to the portal. We should be there in two, maybe three days, depending on how fast we move."

Vicky laughed and took another drink.

"What's so funny?" Ian asked, offended.

"You're so optimistic." Vicky passed the canteen to Antoine. "Only two, maybe three days to go."

"I didn't say *only*."

"It was implied. You've always seen the bright side of every aspect of this journey. I wish I had your outlook."

"Thanks." Ian's anger quickly drained away. "I have to be optimistic. But in the back of my mind I always realize that things could easily get worse."

XIU BROUGHT HER horse to a stop and raised her right hand, warning Lihua to do the same. They had topped the crest of a small hill, only to find that the Sataners had paused on the opposite slope. Her and Lihua backtracked down the hill and waited. When no one raised any alarms or came after them, they tied their horses to a nearby tree and climbed the hill on foot, this time more cautiously. Near the top, they went prone and crawled to the crest on their hands and knees.

Xiu raised her binoculars and scanned the Sataners. After several seconds, she spotted the outsiders. They were lashed to horses and shared a canteen. The four were dirty, haggard, and tired, yet still appeared in good shape. So far, the Sataners had pretty much remained on course.

"What now?" Lihua asked.

"Once the Sataners set out, we'll mark a tree and fo—"

The cocking of a weapon cut off their conversation. Five Sataners stood behind them. Four held Type 63 automatic rifles, while the closest, a woman with a three-inch scar down her cheek, pointed a 9mm Makarov at Xiu.

"Get up!" Scarface waved the pistol. "Place your weapons on the ground and your hands behind your head. Both of you."

Xiu and Zhen did as they were told.

Scarface snapped her fingers to get the attention of one of the gunmen. "Get their horses and weapons."

Stepping closer to the two women, Scarface motioned with the Makarov toward the rest of the Sataners. "Go."

Xiu hesitated. Scarface shoved the pistol into her face. "Now!"

With a deep sigh, Xiu and Lihua topped the hill and headed down the opposite slope.

MEI MEANDERED AROUND the rest spot, desperately trying not to glance toward the hill where her guards said they had spotted someone spying on them. She told Huan to take four armed men and check on the situation. Five tense minutes had passed with no sign of Huan. Finally, one of her guards called out, "They found something."

Mei walked over as the small group descended the hill. They met at the base of the slope.

"I told you I saw someone," said Huan.

"Good job." Mei walked around the two captured women. "You're Unbelievers."

"We're *Xiongnu*," Xiu responded defiantly.

"Why are you following us?"

Neither woman replied.

"What do you want me to do with them?" asked Huan.

Mei ignored her subordinate, instead studying the two intruders. The Unbelievers had avoided them for the past few months, having been cowed in too many confrontations. So, what changed? Why risk an encounter with them no—

Mei chastised herself for being so naïve. She had assumed the rest of the travelers had been killed by the giant worms or in the dust storm when some of them most likely had survived and must be looking for their friends. If the Unbelievers were interested in the travelers, then it indicated that the two groups had joined forces to close the Gate to Salvation.

Mei rushed over to her deputy. "We have to get to the gate as quickly as possible. Give the outsiders their horses back, bind their hands, and make certain the animals are under our control. We're going to double time."

"Yes, ma'am."

As the deputy raced off to complete his orders, Huan gestured toward Xiu and Lihua. "What do you want me to do with these two?"

Mei sneered. "We'll give them a message to send to the Unbelievers."

CHAPTER THIRTY-SIX

THE DEMON HUNTERS and the *Xiongnu* had rested until late afternoon, had a quick dinner, and set out along the G1 shortly after sunset. They had traveled for six hours and, according to the road signs, were approaching the small city Tieling. Qiang stopped the column.

Jason rode his horse up alongside Qiang. "Are we taking a break?"

"No. We're here."

"Where the portal is?"

Qiang pointed west. "The gate is two miles in that direction. You said you wanted to attack during daylight, and this as close as we can get to it without too much of a risk of being discovered. The patrols are going to stay posted so nothing stumbles upon us and will join us at sunrise."

"Thanks."

"I can take you to it if you want. It might help us plan our attack."

"Of course." Jason turned to his team. "Haneef, Ustagov, Father Belsario, Sasha. You're with me. Sook-kyoung, please take care of Lucifer and Lilith until I get back."

Qiang ordered Min to gather up five horsemen. When they were ready, the *Xiongnu* led the way off the G1 toward the portal.

CHAPTER THIRTY-SEVEN

ZHEN HAD A tough time picking up Xiu's trail. After passing her intelligence on to Qiang, she had backtracked to the location where they had found the Sataners and proceeded in the same direction the caravan had gone. At first, she easily spotted the large white X marks that Xiu had chalked onto the trees. However, after crossing a particularly large expanse of abandoned agricultural land, she found nothing. Zhen had been careful when crossing the field not to stray off course; however, when she reached the woods on the opposite side, she could not see any markings. She rode several hundred feet to the left and right in case her bearings had been off, yet still could find no indication as in what direction to go. Zhen was about to turn around when she stumbled across a white X scrawled on the wall of a dilapidated wooden shed inside the woods. She followed the path.

Unfortunately, Zhen came across no other markings for the next hour. The lack of information frustrated her and slowed her efforts to catch up with the others. She considered back-tracking through the woods when she broke through the tree line.

A quarter of a mile away, a small hill rose in front of her. A large fire burned on the reverse slope, illuminating the dark and sending embers churning into the sky. Zhen stopped her horse and listened for the sounds associated with a camp, but she only heard the crackling of the flames. Zhen made her way to the base of the hill, unslung her QBZ-95B carbine, and spurred her horse up the slope. As she reached the crest, she raised her weapon into the high ready position, prepared for anything.

Zhen expected to find a Sataners camp site. Instead, two wooden posts ten feet high had been planted in the soil with a large piece of cloth draped between them. The campfire, or more accurately a bonfire, stood on the opposite side of the makeshift structure. She scanned the area for signs of life and detected none. Using the heels of her boots to nudge her horse in the side, she urged the animal down the slope. When Zhen circled around to the other side of the structure, she leaned forward and vomited.

The wooden posts were the vertical boards of inverted crosses mounted into the ground. Xiu and Lihua had been stripped naked and crucified upside down, with rusted railroad ties hammered through their feet, wrists, and mouths to hold them in place. Each woman had her throat slit so deeply their spines were visible, and their abdomens had been sliced from pelvis to ribcage, allowing the internal organs to fall out and drape onto the dirt. The piece of cloth stretched between the two crucifixes bore four words written in blood.

You can't stop us

BOOK THREE

CHAPTER THIRTY-EIGHT

"**T**HERE IT IS." Qiang pointed down the hill.

Jason did not need to have the portal pointed out to him. By now, he had become all too familiar with them. It sat in an open field that once had been farmland. This one was slightly larger than the others. From this distance, he estimated its diameter at eighty to ninety feet. A rolling black cloud formed the circumference and its surface shimmered like a mirage. A mile to the south stood the camp for the Sataners comprised of larger, more permanent tents. Only a handful of people tended to the site; the main body of the cult had not arrived yet, as Jason had counted on. Except for this hillock, a half mile distant and to the right of the portal, the surrounding land lay flat for several miles. They would not be able to sneak up on this one undetected as they had in Paris and Moscow. On the plus side, so much open space provided them with plenty of room to maneuver. They were going to need it.

An army of Demon Spawn guarded this portal. Five Golem formed a circle around the portal, one behind, two in front, and one on either side, standing close enough together to prevent anyone from getting near the opening. A horde of flesh eaters wandered aimlessly. Naked, emaciated, and with leathery gray skin dried out from the fires of Hell, these were the bodies of those condemned to the Underworld. These demons were slow and uncoordinated, so dealing with one or two was easy. However, a horde of flesh eaters this size could strip a man to the bones in minutes. Much more dangerous were the demons wandering amongst them. Jason recognized the gray, bat-like bodies and bulbous, eyeless heads of soul vampires, the creatures that fed off the souls of humans and spewed acid slime. He had been battling them since the early days of the apocalypse. Even more disturbing was the presence of ravagers, which they first ran across in Siberia. Human in form, with blood red eyes and talons for fingers, these were by far the most dangerous demons yet encountered. They could tear apart a person in seconds and, despite the severity of any wound inflicted upon them, could regenerate in minutes.

The two decimators that had butchered the villagers sat on their haunches on either flank of the demons. When a flesh eater strayed too far from the group, one of the decimators bolted from its position and rushed it. A two-second blur of activity blocked the view and then the decimator returned to its position, leaving behind a pile of severed body parts. The show of force had the desired effect, and the rest of the Demon Spawn closed ranks.

Min shook his head. "How many demons do you think are down there?"

"It's hard to tell," Ustagov answered. "I count eight ravagers and eleven soul vampires."

"How many flesh eaters?" Haneef asked.

Father Belsario lowered his binoculars. "At least three hundred."

Sasha reached out and placed her hand on Jason's shoulder. "This is the toughest we've faced so far."

"This is nothing," said Qiang. "Check out what's on the other side of the gate."

Jason shifted his attention toward the portal. His spirits sank. The familiar blood red sky and gray, barren landscape was covered by scores of Demon Spawn, mostly Golem, ravagers, and soul vampires, which stretched to the horizon. They were not interested in crossing over into this realm. Their presence and numbers bothered Jason.

As the group watched, a sixth Golem approached from the

south, the one created in the decimation field several days previous. It lumbered past the Sataners' camp and made its way through the Demon Spawn. The ravagers and soul vampires moved aside for the behemoth, as did most of the flesh eaters. A few of the latter did not move fast enough to get out its way and were either swatted aside by its meaty hands, their bodies emitting blue eddies of energy as their lifeless forms crashed into the dirt, or were crushed beneath its massive feet. The demon made its way to the portal and joined the other Golem.

"Have there always been this many Demon Spawn here?" Ustagov asked.

Qiang shook his head. "Demons have always hovered around the gate, just never this many. Those on the other side weren't there before."

The doctor chuckled. "It seems our reputation proceeds us."

Sasha leaned closer to Jason so as not to be heard. "You know I'm with you a hundred percent, but there's no way we'll get past all those Demon Spawn."

"I hate to be pessimistic," added Father Belsario. "I agree with Sasha. We're not going to close that portal unless you have one Hell of an ingenious plan."

Jason lowered his binoculars. "It just so happens I do."

THREE HOURS LATER back at the *Xiongnu* campsite, the group stood around Jason who knelt on the ground and outlined the details of the plan he had formulated, using a makeshift map of the portal site drawn in the sand. For the upcoming battle, they would be divided into four sections. Qiang would lead most of the *Xiongnu* into battle against the Demon Spawn and distract them while the Demon Hunters attempted to close the portal. To accomplish that, the latter would divide themselves into two groups; Jason, Haneef, Sasha, and Sook-kyoung would carry one of the antimatter devices and Father Belsario, Gabriel, and Matthew the second. Ustagov would stay back with the remaining device under the protection of five *Xiongnu* horsemen. As Jason laid out his plan, he could tell by their facial expressions and arms crossed over their chests that the others were highly skeptical. When he finished, he stood and brushed the dirt off his knees.

"What do you think?"

No one responded.

"If someone has a better idea, now's the time to speak up."

Father Belsario spoke first. "It's risky."

"It's the only option we have."

The others nodded in reluctant agreement.

"It's the same rules as always," continued Jason. "If the person carrying the device gets taken down, someone else grabs and deploys it. The same goes for the *Xiongnu*. If something happens to us, one of your horsemen will have to finish the job."

"None of us know how to use them," said Qiang.

"They work automatically. All you need to do is throw it into the portal. Once it touches the surface, the device will blast it shut."

"Make certain none of your people touch the portal while deploying the device," said Ustagov.

"Why?"

"It's a one-way portal. Demons can exit Hell into our realm. If anything tries to go in the other direction, it'll instantly be destroyed."

"I'll let them know."

"Then it's settled." Jason paused to give anyone a final chance to weigh in. No one did. "Qiang, brief your people on the plan. The rest of you make any last-minute preparations. I want to be back at the portal shortly after sunrise, so we leave in ten minutes."

As everyone went off to get ready, Jason headed for the tent the *Xiongnu* had set up for him. Lucifer and Lilith waited inside, cuddled together on a blanket that someone had spread out. The werehounds jumped up at the sight of their master and rushed him. Jason crouched in front of them and received a double face bath.

Less than two minutes later, the flap to his tent opened, and Sasha stepped in. Jason scratched the two werehounds behind the ears and stood. "Was there something about the plan—"

Sasha slid her hands across Jason's cheeks, cupped them around the back of his head, and pulled him toward her. Her lips pressed against his in a kiss filled with as much passion as affection. She broke away after several seconds, keeping her hands behind his head and running her fingers through his hair.

"I love you. I've loved you since we first met at Mont St. Michel, only then I was too stupid to admit it to myself, and I lost you. I'm not trying to take you away from Jeanette and, even if I could, I'm not supposed to become involved with you. There's a good chance you might not make it through this morning, and I can't bear the thought of not telling you how I feel."

"Don't worry. Everyth—"

Sasha kissed him again, her lips warmer and more inviting this time. When she broke the embrace, she placed her forehead against his and whispered, "Don't say anything. Just accept that I love you."

Sasha rushed out of the tent, leaving Jason alone with his emotions and two werehounds who tilted their heads and stared at him in confusion.

CHAPTER THIRTY-NINE

MEI HAD MADE her group travel through the night with only two brief rest stops. The sparsity of breaks did not affect Jeanette much because Mei had not allowed them to eat or drink anything since the forced march began. Thankfully, they did not have to walk tied up as they had in the earlier part of the trip; otherwise they would have collapsed hours ago. After riding in a saddle for so long, her legs, lower back, and butt ached. Jeanette did not let the discomfort bother her. She knew what Mei had in store would be infinitely more painful.

The sun crested the eastern horizon. Its rays stretched across the landscape, creating long shadows from those objects in its path. Jeanette lowered her head to one side to avoid the intense light shining in her eyes.

On her right, Antoine whispered, "Hey."

"What?"

"I think we've arrived at wherever these lunatics are taking us."

Jeanette shaded the sun with her right hand. A quarter of a mile ahead of them stood a more permanent camp, the tents larger and better constructed than those used while traveling the countryside, especially one in the center three times the size of the others. Fire pits and cooking stations had been set up and toilet facilities built along the western perimeter. She figured this was Mei's home base. Her suspicions were confirmed when Ian called out, "There she is, mates."

Jeanette leaned to one side. A mile beyond the camp was the portal. Hundreds of demons stood between them and the portal, too many for her to count, although even at this distance she could detect several Golem standing guard.

"What have we gotten ourselves into?" Vicky muttered.

Ian chuckled. "A bloody fine mess."

Antoine maneuvered his horse closer to Jeanette, although not enough to bring attention onto him. He whispered, "Let me know when you want to make a break for it."

She lifted her tied hands in front of her. "How?"

Antoine raised his a few inches out of his lap. He pulled his wrists aside, showing that the knot had been loosened. "I've been working on them all night. Just say when."

Jeanette nodded.

As they approached the camp, the flaps on the large tent in the center opened. Bai exited and made her way through the compound. The decimators left their spot on either side of the horde and joined her. Mei ordered the caravan to stop. She dismounted and stood by her horse. As Bai approached, Mei bowed deeply.

"You arrived sooner than I anticipated, my child."

"I'm afraid there are more travelers trying to close the Gate to Salvation."

A sinister expression spread across Bai's face. "I'm sure there are."

"You're not concerned?"

"Why should I be?" Bai stretched her arms wide toward the portal, reminding Jeanette of Christ on the crucifix. "I have a legion of the Blessed protecting us. What do I have to fear from mortals such as these?"

Mei lowered her head, an expression of dejection twisting her features. Bai ran a talon down the woman's cheek, a twisted gesture of affection.

"Don't despair, my child. You are mortal, too. You have seen the Darkness and have accepted it, and as such you are saved."

"Thank you, my Mistress." Mei motioned toward Jeanette.

"Should I prepare them for the ritual?"

"There's been a change in plans. Satan wants to talk to them personally."

"Of course, my Mistress." Mei bowed and waited for Bai to wander off. "Get the travelers ready."

Several of Mei's people approached. Antoine quietly asked, "Now?"

"Not yet."

Jeanette and the others were helped off their horses and herded to an open area in front of the camp with a direct line of sight to the portal. Mei stood in front of Jeanette. "Please kneel before our Dark Lord and Master."

When Jeanette refused, Mei nodded. One of the guards moved up behind Jeanette. He pushed down on her left shoulder with one hand while shoving his foot against the back of her lower left calf. Jeanette dropped onto the dirt, grimacing when her knees hit the ground. Mei stepped toward the others. For a moment, Jeanette thought Antoine might lunge. Instead, he sought guidance from Jeanette. She motioned with her head for him to kneel, and he obliged. Ian and Vicky did the same.

Mei and the rest of the Sataners stepped away, congregating a hundred yards ahead. Two of the group stayed behind to guard the Demon Hunters, taking up position a few feet to their rear. Mei's people gathered around Bai and prostrated themselves around her, bowing toward the portal. Ahead of them, the Demon Spawn grew agitated.

"What's going on?" Vicky asked.

"I don't know," said Jeanette, trying to conceal the rising fear in her voice.

"Whatever it is, mate," said Ian, "it can't be anything good."

CHAPTER FORTY

THE DEMON HUNTERS and *Xiongnu* arrived at the portal, using the opposite slope of the hillock to shield their presence. Jason, Sasha, Ustagov, Father Belsario, and Qiang climbed to the top to survey the situation one final time before launching their attack. A frenetic level of activity took place below, especially among the Demon Spawn.

"That can't be good," said Qiang.

"It doesn't change anything," Father Belsario responded.

Jason scanned the area between the portal and the Sataners' camp with his binoculars. The mass of cultists prostrating themselves around the Seamstress drew his attention. Behind them, four figures knelt in the dirt. Two men with Type 63 automatic rifles guarded them. Jason recognized Jeanette and the others. "Damn it."

"What's wrong?" asked Father Belsario.

"The Sataners are already here. And the Seamstress and our missing people are with them."

"How many?" Sasha shifted her binoculars to the left.

"All of them."

Sasha zoomed in, checking to make sure their people were all right, and then focused on the Sataners. "I wonder what has them and the Demon Spawn all worked up."

Ustagov pointed to the portal. "I guess it's that."

The others turned their attention toward it. Father Belsario mumbled a silent prayer. Jason could only say, "You've got to be kidding me."

What approached from the Hell side of the portal was

nothing short of a living nightmare. Human in shape, it stood forty feet tall, twice the size of the Golem. Fin-shaped scales protruded vertically in a line along both arms from the elbow to the wrist and divided along the top of its hands, ending at the fingertips in jagged talons. A twenty-foot long tail swirled behind the demon, the tip bulbous and covered in spike-shaped scales. Its head was elongated, ending in a jaw filled with rows of fangs. Blood-red eyes set deep back in its skull glowed from the shadow of its sockets. Two horns protruded from where the ears should be; they ran half-way down the side of its head before curling up and back, the tips ending near the back of its skull. It was dark crimson in color.

"Is that who I think it is?" Jason asked.

"If it is, we're screwed." Ustagov lowered his binoculars.

The creature, still more than half a mile from the portal, moved at an excruciatingly slow pace. One leg would lumber forward, its hoof smashing into the ground. Several seconds later, the other massive leg would move. With each step, Demon Spawn would surge to the sides, creating a path for the creature. At this rate, it would be a good fifteen to twenty minutes before it reached the opening.

Jason lowered his binoculars and rolled onto his side to talk to the others. "If we move now, we should have enough time to close the portal before it gets here."

Father Belsario raised an eyebrow. "We need to change the plans to include rescuing our people."

"We don't have time," said Jason. "They'll have to fend for themselves until we deploy the device."

Sasha placed her hand on Jason's wrist. "Let me take Lucifer and Lilith and go rescue them."

"You have the device."

"I can deploy it," said Father Belsario. "What Sasha says makes sense. It at least gives them a fighting chance and doesn't hurt our odds of success."

Jason thought for a moment. "Okay. Free Jeanette and the

others and then take on the Sataners and cover our back."

Sasha nodded.

Jason crawled down the opposite slope. "We launch our attack in two minutes."

CHAPTER FORTY-ONE

"**I** CAN'T BELIEVE it." Mei could barely contain her excitement. "The Arrival has finally come."

Bai flashed her a look of disdain.

Mei heard a commotion nearby. At first, she thought her followers were expressing similar enthusiasm. Then she heard the pounding of hooves followed by the chirping of ravagers. She lifted herself off the ground as a cavalry of horsemen topped the crest of the hill to their right and descended the slope. Mei expected the marauders to raid the camp. Instead, the horsemen charged directly into the Demon Spawn.

"The Unbelievers are here," said Mei. "What should we do?"

"Stop them, you little fool," Bai answered.

Mei bowed her head in shame for appearing weak in front of Bai. Humiliation morphed into anger at those who dared to intrude on this sacred event. Mei shouted, "Kill the intruders!"

QIANG LED THE charge. Like the other *Xiongnu*, he had his bow loaded and ready to fire. The unanticipated presence of the Sataners posed a threat to his left flank; he would have to deal with that. If luck stayed with him, he might be able to use the Sataners to his advantage. For the moment, he concentrated on his target—the horde of demons directly in front of him.

The flesh eaters heard the stampeding horses and shifted in their direction. Qiang ignored them. They posed little threat to his horsemen. He focused on those from the Underworld since they were the biggest danger. As anticipated, upon the approach of the humans, the ravagers and soul vampires rushed toward the horsemen.

The *Xiongnu* raised their bows and aimed.

JEANETTE FELT A sense of anticipation flow through her when the horsemen crested the hill. She had no clue who they were, or whether they were friend or foe. They distracted the Sataners, which gave her and the others a fighting chance, no matter how slim it may be.

She nodded to Antoine. He had already swung into action, slipping off the ropes from around his wrist. The closest guard stood five feet behind him, his weapon clutched in his right hand and not ready to be fired, his attention drawn to the commotion on the nearby hillock. Jumping to his feet and spinning around, Antoine lunged at and collided with the much smaller man, throwing him back onto the ground and knocking the wind out of him. Before the guard could catch his breath, Antoine fell on him, pinning the automatic rifle to the ground with his right knee while pummeling the Sataner with his fists.

The second guard raised his Type 63 and aimed at Antoine's back. Jeanette jumped to her feet. Because her hands were still bound in front of her, she could not move easily and stumbled. Spotting the movement in his peripheral vision, the guard stepped to the side, raised his weapon level with his head, and slammed the stock into Jeanette's face. As she toppled over, the guard raised his weapon, aimed at Antoine's back, and squeezed the—

A dark blur came out of nowhere and rammed into the guard, throwing him three feet into the air. He hit the ground hard. Before he could react, Lilith lunged at him again, pinning him with her body. He flung his arms, trying to punch the werehound, stopping when she morphed into her demonic form. The guard's screams of terror were cut short when Lilith plunged the stinger of her scorpion-like tail into his chest and pumped him with paralyzing fluid.

Jeanette jumped when she felt something brush up against her. She lifted her head as Lucifer licked her face. If they were here, Jason must be nearby.

A moment later, Sasha rode up on her horse. She slid out of the saddle, rushed over to Jeanette, and used her saber to cut through the bonds.

"I never thought I'd say this," Jeanette said, "I'm glad to see you."

Sasha chuckled.

The knot fell apart. As Jeanette rubbed her wrists, Sasha rushed over to the guard Lilith had immobilized. Pausing long enough to scratch the werehound behind her scaly ears, she grabbed the guard's automatic rifle and shoulder bag of magazines. Antoine had taken the other guard's weapon and untied Ian and Vicky.

"What do we do now?" asked the Moroccan.

"What we do best." Sasha smiled. "Protect Jason's ass while he closes the portal."

QIANG WATCHED THE ravagers and soul vampires as they closed the distance with the *Xiongnu*. When within range, his horsemen released a barrage of more than sixty arrows into the approaching creatures. Most hit their target, taking out or incapacitating five ravagers and six soul vampires. Eight were left unscathed. The remaining demons made their way through the horde and ripped eight of Qiang's people out of their saddles, the men's screams of terror and pain drowned out by the charging horses. The five soul vampires stayed behind, taking the opportunity to drain the souls from their victims. The three ravagers spun around and pursued the horsemen.

The *Xiongnu* had already reloaded their bows and released another barrage at the flesh eaters. Close to fifty went down as the arrows punctured their skulls, sending blue eddies of energy drifting skyward. A few seconds later, the *Xiongnu* reached the flesh eaters. The horses were traveling so fast they plowed their way through the demons, pushing them aside or trampling them underfoot. Enough of the soulless wanderers swarmed them that three *Xiongnu* were torn from their saddles, dragged to the ground, and devoured. A ravager caught up with the last horsemen in line and leaped, taking down both the animal and its rider.

Once Qiang had reached the center of the horde, he steered his horsemen left. They burst through the southern fringes and headed for the Sataners, with the surviving ravagers in pursuit.

"IT WORKED." FATHER Belsario watched from the crest of the hillock as the *Xiongnu* distracted the Demon Spawn's attention away from the portal.

"I figured it would. Let's hope the Golem are as accommodating." Jason placed a hand on Ustagov's shoulder. "You know what to do?"

The doctor tapped the saddle bag containing the antimatter device and nodded. "Good luck."

"Thanks." Jason reached out and clasped the doctor's hand. "You'll need it as much as we do."

Jason and Father Belsario headed down to where the others waited with the horses, leaving Ustagov and Hong monitoring events from the summit. They mounted their horses. Jason maneuvered his over to the cleric. "The same goes for you. Good luck."

"God sent me here to help you fight the Demon Spawn. Let's hope he's got our backs on this one."

Jason spurred on his horse, and the others fell in line behind him. The Demon Hunters rounded the northern tip of the hill and charged the Golem guarding the portal.

MEI DIRECTED HER people to fire on the Unbelievers when a young woman beside her asked, "What about those from the Underworld?"

"Don't worry about hitting them. They don't matter."

"I don't mean that." The young woman pointed in front of her. "They're heading toward us."

Mei directed her attention to the horde. The Unbelievers had charged into them before changing direction toward the camp, leading the creatures directly to them. "We have to stop the *Xiongnu*. Fire when you're ready."

A gunshot rang out. A moment later, Mei heard the sickening thud of a bullet striking flesh. The young woman's skull exploded, splattering Mei with bone fragments and chunks of gore. A teenage boy to her left cried out as a bullet punctured his spine. He was dead before he hit the ground. A third shot whizzed past, missing Mei's head by inches. The prisoners had overcome the guards, stolen their weapons, and were using them on her people. Two dogs and a figure dressed in a red cloak had joined them. A flash of gunfire came from one of the stolen weapons and a middle-aged woman beside Mei took a bullet to the heart.

"The prisoners have broken loose." Mei shouted to be heard over the noise. "Half of you defend our rear."

Bai stepped forward and clutched Mei's upper arm with such force it sent a bolt of pain down her arm. "You worry about the Unbelievers. I'll take care of this nuisance."

Bai made her way toward the prisoners, with the decimators on either flank. Mei focused her attention back on the charging horses. The soul vampires had finished feeding off their victims and were chasing after the Unbelievers on a path that would take them right through her own people.

SASHA AND ANTOINE lay prone, their cheeks resting on the stock of the Type 63s as they centered the crosshairs on members of the Sataners. The first two rounds had taken down their targets with a single shot. After that, Mei's people got wise and sought cover, making it more difficult for Sasha and Antoine to register a kill. As long as Mei's people avoided getting shot, they posed no threat to the *Xiongnu*.

Lilith crouched behind Sasha. She growled, a deep guttural sound that signified danger.

"What's up, girl?"

"We have company." Jeanette pointed to their left. Bai approached, her gait slow and menacing, her gaze focused on the Demon Hunters. The decimators kept pace a few feet to her rear.

"What do you want me to do?" Antoine asked.

Sasha thought for a moment. "Shift fire to the decimators. And make every shot count."

JASON LED THE charge toward the portal. Haneef stayed to his right and Sook-kyoung to his left. The two closest Golem spotted them and shifted their stance, their massive bodies positioned to block the humans. As the Demon Hunters Gaters drew near, each Golem raised its right arm across its chest. At the last second, the horses veered left. The two creatures swung, missing their targets by more than ten feet.

The three stopped fifty feet from the portal, maneuvered their horses sideways, and raised their AK-47s. Jason and Haneef aimed at the nearest Golem's head while Sook-kyoung concentrated on where its heart should be, and emptied their magazines into the Golem. It bellowed in defiance as sixty rounds pulverized its face and head and another thirty shredded its heart. As each round found its mark, Jason detected the aura of a trapped soul expressing relief from its hellish confines. When all three magazines had been used, the Golem staggered, two-thirds of its head blasted away and blood oozing from the gaping hole in its chest. It dropped to its knees and fell forward, crashing into the ground with a loud thud.

As Jason and the others reloaded, the second Golem surged toward them.

THE *XIONGNU* CLOSED the distance with the Sataners. Qiang's people leaned forward against their horses' necks to diminish their target profile. Not that they needed to. The Sataners' aim was panicked and ineffective. Only nine of his people went down, most of those because the riders' horses were hit.

When within range, the *Xiongnu* sat back up, raised the bows, and released a barrage of arrows. Half found their targets, killing or wounding twenty-one Sataners. The gunfire tapered off to a few stray rounds. The *Xiongnu* loosed a second barrage, taking down eighteen more. The gunfire ceased entirely. A few seconds later, the *Xiongnu* reached the Sataners and broke through their line. Horses trampled humans underfoot or pushed them out of the way. What little resistance remained shattered, and the surviving Sataners threw aside their weapons and ran for the safety of their camp.

They had covered only a few yards when the ravagers and soul vampires arrived. In the confusion of battle, and with the Seamstress preoccupied and unable to issue orders, the demons were unable to distinguish ally from enemy. They sensed the fear of the Sataners and were driven into a frenzy by the adrenalin rush. Food fleeing on foot made for easier prey than that mounted on horses.

The ravagers and soul vampires switched targets and descended on the Sataners.

THE *XIONGNU* SPLIT into two groups. Qiang led half the horsemen and circled back around, charging the retreating Sataners and Demon Spawn. Min led the rest against the Seamstress.

THE BOLT ON Sasha's Type 63 stuck open, signifying her weapon was out of ammunition. She had emptied two entire magazines into the approaching decimators without effect. Reaching into the ammunition bag, she rummaged around for full magazines, finding one of the last two. Sasha popped out the empty and slammed in the new one.

"I'm almost out," she yelled. "I've got only one magazine left after this."

Antoine's Type 63 expended its ammunition. He reached into his bag and removed the remaining full magazine. "This is my last."

Ian grunted. "That's not good, mate."

HOW PITIFUL THESE humans are, thought Bai. *As if their mortal weapons could affect the likes of me. Their deaths will be painful and merciless, a lesson to anyone who attempts to stop the Dark Lord's will.*

Bai prepared to unleash the decimators when screams emanated from behind her. The *Xiongnu* horsemen broke through the Sataners' lines, scattering Mei's people. Typical of humans: strong in faith, lacking in courage. The fact that ravagers and soul vampires ripped through them caused her little distress. If these humans served as food for her minions, then at least they were of some use. She was more concerned with the twenty horsemen bearing down on her.

Snapping her fingers to get the decimators' attention, Bai pointed to the approaching horsemen.

"Tear them apart."

JASON FINISHED RELOADING his AK-47 when he saw the Golem only a few yards away.

"Watch out."

Haneef and Sook-kyoung had already retreated. The Golem swung, missing by scant feet. It lumbered toward the humans, determined to rid itself of them. The three fell back fifty feet, aimed their weapons at its head and heart, and fired. The Golem raised its arms in front of its face and chest, allowing the bullets to thud harmlessly into its meaty forearms.

Before the Golem could respond, the Purgatoriati rode up behind it. Gabriel and Matthew dismounted before their horses came to a complete stop, unsheathing their broadswords as they did. Gabriel slashed his blade across the demon's left Achilles' tendon. Matthew plunged his upwards through the Golem's back, the tip puncturing several of its hearts. The Golem spun to its left, hoping to swat away its attackers. When it applied pressure to its left leg, the demon's ankle gave out and it toppled over. Father Belsario rushed forward and drove his broadsword through its left temple and twisted the hilt in a circular motion, scrambling the demon's brains. The Golem went limp.

Three more Golem left their positions and lumbered toward the attackers. The fourth shifted its position to stand directly in front of the portal.

ON THE OTHER side, Satan had approached to within five hundred feet of the portal.

USTAGOV AND THE five *Xiongnu* watched from the top of the hill as the battle played out. Hong pointed toward the portal.

"It's getting closer."

Ustagov assessed that the monstrosity would reach the opening in less than five minutes. He headed down the opposite slope toward the horses.

"Where are you going?" Hong asked.

"We have to get out of here now."

"I won't leave the others."

"I don't have time to explain." Ustagov grabbed his horse's

reins and climbed into the saddle. "If we wait any longer, it'll be too late."

"I won't abandon my duty."

"Your duty is to protect me."

"I'm not a coward. I won't run away."

"Suit yourself." Spurring on his horse, Ustagov rode off past the northern slope of the hillock with the portal to his left.

THE *XIONGNU* HAD closed to within one hundred feet of the Sataners and rampaging demons when Qiang held up his hand and ordered them to stop.

"What are you doing?" one of his horsemen asked. "We have them on the run."

"I know," said Qiang. "Let the demons take care of them. It'll be a fitting punishment."

MEI CHECKED OVER her shoulder as she ran for her tent. She wet herself at what she witnessed.

A soul vampire pounced onto the teenager nearest her, knocking him off his feet and pinning him to the ground. The young man managed to roll over and punch the demon several times in what should have been its face, each blow having no effect. It screeched in defiance and regurgitated its acid vomit onto the teenager's head. His features melted, the vomitus dissolving the skin and eyes and eating its way through the skull. He screamed maniacally, the fear and pain having torn away his sanity, until the acid burned away his tongue and vocal cords.

To Mei's right, a ravager raced past a middle-aged woman, swinging a taloned claw across her left leg and severing the limb below the knee. She toppled forward, her cry of agony becoming muted as she collapsed face-first onto the ground. The first ravager circled around in front of the humans and double backed, launching into a flying leap and taking down the young woman to Mei's left. A second ravager pounced onto the crippled middle-aged woman and slashed open her back.

Something approached Mei from behind. A soul vampire lunged, landing on and pushing her over. Mei's back slammed into the dirt, knocking the wind out of her. She barely felt the demon climb onto her chest or pin down her shoulders. The only indication Mei had of her imminent death was when she smelled the acid rising in the demon's throat.

MIN NOTICED THE Seamstress pointing out his horsemen to the decimators. It suddenly dawned on him what was about to happen. Before he could warn his men, the twin demons morphed into a blur. One reappeared over the horseman to Min's left. He heard a momentary cry, and two seconds later the blur moved on. The horse and rider continued charging, sliced asunder but held together by perpetual motion, like a hideous puzzle. After a moment, the two beings fell apart, collapsing to the dirt and somersaulting into a pile of organs and tissue. Behind him, Min heard similar cries.

"Split up," he yelled. "It's your only chance."

THE BOLT ON Sasha's AK-47 locked in the open position. The Seamstress drew closer, her gait slow and menacing. Thankfully, the decimators had gone after other prey.

Vicky ran over to one of the dead Sataners and pulled aside his coat. He had a machete tied to his right leg.

"What are you doing?" asked Ian.

"Trying to find weapons." Vicky pulled the machete from its scabbard and tossed it in front of Jeanette. She frisked the body and, upon finding nothing of value, moved on to the next. Discovering a four-inch knife, Vicky removed the weapon and held it above her head. "Any takers?"

Ian stepped over. "Are you sure you don't want it?"

"Hand to hand combat is not my thing." Vicky passed the knife to Ian and picked up the spare Type 63.

Ian stepped alongside Antoine, who held his Type 63 in such a manner to use the stock as a weapon.

Jeanette picked up the machete. She twirled it in her hand, getting a feel for the blade. Once familiar with it, she lowered her hands to her sides. "Let's do this. That bitch is mine."

"Correction." Sasha moved up beside Jeanette, the saber raised in front of her. Lucifer and Lilith stood on either side, already morphed into their demonic forms. "The bitch is *ours*."

AS LONG AS they kept enough distance between themselves and the Golem, Jason knew his people were in little danger. He worried about Father Belsario, however. The cleric and his two Purgatoriati stayed close to the demons, taunting and distracting them to give the others a clear shot. When one spun around and swiped at Matthew, Sook-kyoung raised her AK-47 and emptied her magazine into the back of its head. It howled and collapsed to its knees. Matthew rushed forward and drove his broadsword into the demon's face between its eyes. The Golem hovered for a moment and toppled forward. Matthew barely got out of the way in time.

One Golem attempted to keep an eye on all the humans; there were too many. Movement to the right caught its attention. It reached out as a rider-less horse rushed past. The Golem caught the animal by its neck, lifting it off the ground. The horse bucked so hard it shattered its own spine, going limp in the Golem's hand. As Gabriel rushed toward it, the Golem flung the horse at him. The carcass slammed into his chest, throwing him back fifteen feet. His ribs fractured and several organs ruptured. Gabriel lay dazed and confused, unaware the demon moved toward him until it picked him up by his legs. The Golem wrapped its other hand around Gabriel's torso and pulled. He screamed as an unbearable pain washed over him. A moment later, Gabriel's body tore along his waist. His internal organs spilled out from under his cloak, piling up at the Golem's feet. The demon tossed the legs toward Jason and Sook-kyoung, covering them in blood. The torso he flung at Father Belsario, forcing him to duck.

Rather than press their attack, the surviving Golem fell back and joined the other demon guarding the portal, forming a semi-circle fifty feet in diameter in front of the portal, blocking anyone from getting close.

Jason and the others moved in to clear a path.

Satan was less than two hundred feet from the opening.

USTAGOV HAD TRAVELED a quarter of a mile from the battlefield when he steered his horse around and headed back, approaching the portal from behind.

WHEN BAI APPROACHED to thirty feet, Sasha twisted her saber at an angle, ready to strike. "I wouldn't come any closer."

"You have more spirit than the rest of these humans." Bai flashed a sardonic smile, which changed to confusion. She stopped and twisted her head, contemplating Sasha. "You're not like Mei and her flock. You're different."

Lucifer growled and lowered his body, ready to pounce.

"Nor are these earthly animals." Bai studied the were-hounds. "I recognize them as belonging to the Dark Lord's realm. Psychopomps."

Lilith barked.

"It figures such vermin would hang around with someone such as you."

"W-what do you mean?" Sasha stammered.

"It should be obvious, even for you." Bai circled the group, her gait slow and sensuous, like a runway model. "You're not human, nor are you otherworldly like me. You must be one of those pathetic mercenaries recruited from Purgatory to fight your Father's battle for him. Not evil enough to be banished to Hell, yet not good enough to meet His expectations and be granted access to Heaven."

"Stop it," Sasha ordered.

"How does it feel to be rejected by everyone?"

"I said stop it."

Bai's expression became evil. "Even Jason."

"That's enough!" yelled Sasha.

"You're right." Bai raised her right hand and held it palm out toward the group. "Now it's time to die."

"THEY'RE NOT FALLING for it anymore," said Haneef as he attempted to get a good shot at any of the three remaining Golem.

"Keep trying," ordered Jason. "We have to keep them distracted for a few more minutes."

The surviving Golem had learned from the destruction of the others; an ability for which Jason had not given them credit. He had been trying to lure them away from the portal by singling one out for attack, hoping the others would come to its defense. It had worked at first until the last three realized they had left the portal exposed and fell back to defend it. Now, rather than fight the humans, they protected themselves against the attacks. Every time someone fired at a Golem, it would shield its head and chest by covering the vital spots with its arms.

Father Belsario ran up to the Golem on the far right and rammed his broadsword into the demon's left leg, twisting the blade. It cried out and swung at the cleric. Father Belsario anticipated the move and dodged the blow. When the Golem exposed its chest and head, the others opened fire. It tried to block the bullets, but its movements were too slow. They pumped over fifty rounds into the demon before it bellowed and fell over, missing Father Belsario by a few feet. The cleric ran toward the gate. The Golem in the middle, having observed the human approaching from the side, shifted its position to the left and blocked his path.

Jason checked his AK-47. The magazine was empty. "That's it for me. How are you guys fixed?"

"Just a few rounds left," said Haneef.

Sook-kyoung switched out the empty magazine. "Last one. When this is done, we're screwed."

"In more ways than one," Matthew retorted.

Satan had reached the portal and bent over to cross through into their realm.

CHAPTER FORTY-TWO

LUCIFER LUNGED AT Bai, momentarily distracting her. She swung her right hand at the werehound. Ice-blue light washed over the werehound, freezing him in place.

Sasha surged forward. Raising the saber above her head, she brought down the blade on Bai's outstretched arm, severing it below the elbow. The stream of light ended. Lucifer retreated several paces, whining and shaking his head as he recovered. Sasha took five steps back, her saber level and ready to be driven through the Bai's head.

"Had enough?"

Bai laughed. "My child, I've only begun."

She stretched her right arm to the side. The amputated limb vibrated for a moment before levitating off the dirt and reconnecting with the stump. The bone, muscles, and skin melded together. Bai raised her hand and flexed the fingers into a fist.

Jeanette charged. Bai held out her right hand and enveloped the woman in an aura of white light. "Can you hear me, little one?"

"Yes."

"Let's make this interesting." A smirk pierced Bai's lips. "Kill the others."

Sasha sneered. "That's not going to—"

Jeanette sidestepped toward Sasha and swung the machete at her neck. The blade would have sliced Sasha's throat if she had not leaned back at the last second. Before Sasha could regain her footing, Jeanette swung again. Sasha dove to the left, her arm above her head so that she rolled into an upright position behind Jeanette and turned to face the latter's back.

"We can't fight each—"

Jeanette spun around, swinging the machete in a wide arc. Sasha leaned back again, but this time Jeanette lowered the weapon. The blade sliced across Sasha's chest, leaving a gash across her lower abdomen below the breastplate one foot long and two inches deep. Blood flowed from the wound. When Sasha glanced down to check how badly hurt she was, Jeanette cleaved the machete toward her head. Sasha raised the saber above her, the blade stopping the blow. Sasha twisted to the right, deflecting Jeanette's attack and exposing the woman's right flank. She slammed the hilt of her saber against Jeanette's skull, stunning her and opening a gash along her right temple. Stepping back ten feet, Sasha unfastened her cloak and allowed it to slide off her shoulders.

"Jeanette," she pleaded. "Don't do this."

Jeanette staggered, trying to regain her composure.

"She can't hear you," said Bai. "She's under my thrall, and she'll continue to fight until one of you is dead. I'm sure Jason will appreciate the irony."

"When I'm through with Jeanette, I'm going to take you apart piece by piece, you bitch."

"You're too late." Bai stretched out her arms, exposing the numerous sutured sections, and laughed. "I like you. You have spirit. Let's see how you can handle this."

Bai closed her eyes and telepathically called the decimators.

MIN WAITED FOR the inevitable. Most of his men had already been slaughtered by the decimators and nothing he could do would prevent further losses. One moment his horsemen were riding beside him, and the next they were piles of human and animal detritus across the field.

Suddenly, the demons abandoned the massacre and raced

toward the Seamstress. Min had no idea why but was not about to question his good luck. Bringing his horse to a stop, he surveyed the situation. Only four of his horsemen remained, including himself. Maybe he might survive this after all.

When Min focused his attention on the gate, his heart sank.

USTAGOV WAS ONLY five hundred feet from the rear of the portal. He unslung from his shoulder the saddle bag containing the anti-matter device and clutched it in his right hand. The doctor had no idea how the battle progressed because the backside was nothing more than a shimmering dark mass, much like the reverse side of a mirror. However, he could tell by the ungodly sound emanating from the battlefield things were not going well.

MEI CLOSED HER eyes and waited for the soul vampire that pinned her to the ground to spew its acid vomit across her face. When she felt fluid splash against her cheek she screamed. It did not burn, nor did it flow over her as she had expected. Instead, it felt like a dripping sensation. Taking a deep breath to steady her nerves, Mei opened her eyes.

An arrow protruded from the soul vampire's head, entering the back of the skull and exiting through the forehead. The dripping she felt came from the bloody wound. The demon still lived, though its life faded rapidly. Mei placed her hands on its chest, shoving it to one side, and scrambled to her feet. Before she could stand, a hand clutched the collar of her shirt and pulled her upright. Qiang placed his face only inches from hers.

"You're not going anywhere."

The rest of Mei's people had been slaughtered, torn apart by the very demons Bai had sworn would protect them. The Unbelievers now waded through the killing field, finishing off the last of the ravagers and soul vampires.

"Why did you spare me?"

"I didn't," he spat. "You're going to pay for what you did and for all the people you murdered."

A wail echoed across the landscape. Qiang shivered at the sound. Not Mei. She welcomed it. It was the sound of salvation.

IAN SNUCK UP behind Jeanette and wrapped his arms around her, pinning her arms. Jeanette struggled, still too stunned to fight back.

"I've got this," he said to Sasha, and motioned his head toward Bai. "You take care of her."

Sasha nodded and moved in on Bai's right, her saber raised and ready for battle. Antoine and Vicky approached from the other side, each brandishing an automatic rifle to use the stock as a ram.

Sasha attacked first, rushing forward and slicing the saber in a downward stroke. Bai crouched and pivoted. The blade missed her head by inches. As she came out of her pivot, Bai swung her left leg, catching Sasha behind the knees and knocking her legs out from under her. Sasha crashed to the ground, momentarily stunned. Bai stepped over, raised her right leg, and prepared to stomp her foe's head.

Antoine jumped Bai from behind, placing his arm around her neck and pulling her away from Sasha. Bai attempted to break free, unable to due to the Moroccan's strength and her being off balance. Reaching behind her, Bai clutched at him, hoping to claw his eyes. Vicky raced around the front and grabbed Bai's arm. Bai lashed out with her other hand. Taloned fingers slashed across Vicky's face, leaving three gashes down her left temple and cheek. Vicky released her grip and fell back. She wiped her hand across the wound. Blood covered her palm.

Jeanette regained her senses; suddenly aware someone

pinned her arms from behind. She leaned her head forward and brought it back as fast and hard as possible, slamming the back of her skull into Ian's face. He swore as a front tooth fell out and his nose shattered. The bolt of pain caused him to momentarily loosen his grip, which provided the opportunity Jeanette needed. She leaned forward and to the left and slammed her right elbow into Ian's abdomen, knocking the air out of his lungs. His grip loosened. Shoving backward, Jeanette knocked Ian to the ground, spun around, and raised the machete above her head, the blade pointed at his ribcage.

Lucifer tackled Jeanette from the side, knocking her over. She struggled to get back to her feet, but the werehound pinned her, his front paws pressed against her shoulders. Desperate to break free, she hacked at his back with the machete. The blade clicked harmlessly against his scales. Lucifer lowered his head, placed his open jaws over Jeanette's throat, and slowly closed his mouth, applying an increasing amount of pressure. Jeanette continued to struggle until she felt his canines piercing her skin and the fangs pressing against her arteries. She went limp, allowing the machete to fall out of her hand. Lucifer lessened the pressure while keeping his jaws covering Jeanette's throat.

At that moment, the decimators attacked.

The first landed on Lucifer's back. Its taloned claws sliced frantically at its victim, but the scales on the werehound's back saved him from sustaining any wounds. The decimator remained in place and continued slashing ineffectively, its determination making it vulnerable. As Sasha climbed to her feet, she spotted the blurred image on Lucifer's back. Raising the saber above her head, she rushed the werehound.

"Forgive me, boy."

Sasha brought the blade down on top of the blur.

Lucifer yelped, more from fright than pain.

The decimator howled. The blur focused into a sharper image. Sasha had practically cleaved the demon in half, the blade imbedded in its back from its right shoulder down to its lower left abdomen. The mortally-wounded creature crawled off Lucifer and dragged itself toward Bai. Sasha moved up behind the demon and used her foot to pin it to the ground. Grabbing the handle of her saber, she twisted it back and forth until the weapon broke free, then brought the blade down on its neck. The decimator emitted a half-howl before its head rolled across the dirt.

The second decimator attacked Antoine, latching onto his back. He screamed as the talons ripped through flesh and slashed away tissue. Lilith had observed the demon approaching and moved closer. The moment it landed on Antoine, she plunged the stinger into the center of the blur and pumped paralyzing fluid. The accelerated movement stopped, revealing the demon attached to the Moroccan. It hung there for a moment before sliding off. Although the attack had lasted only a second, the damage was fatal. Antoine's left arm had been severed at the shoulder and remained wrapped around Bai's neck; his right arm dangled by his side, held in place by a few tendons. His face and half the skin on his back had been sliced away. The internal organs were exposed through a deep gash in his rear abdomen. Antoine stumbled back from Bai. He opened the gaping hole that used to be his mouth but was in too much pain and shock to speak. A gasp escaped from his throat, followed by a mouthful of frothy blood. Antoine dropped face first onto the ground, a pool of blood forming beneath him and soaking into the soil.

Sasha walked over to the paralyzed decimator. Its eyes followed her movement. She plunged the tip of her saber through its heart and twisted. Its body shuddered once. Raising her foot, she brought the heel down on the decimator's head. The skull ruptured, spitting out blood and gore. Removing the saber from the demon's chest, Sasha swung around to face Bai.

Ian moved up on Sasha's right, clutching the hunting knife in his right hand. He sniffed back the blood dripping down his sinuses and spit it onto the decimator. Vicky picked up the machete Jeanette had attacked them with and joined Sasha on her left.

"It's just the four of us now," said Sasha.

"You are so wrong." Euphoria spread across Bai's face.

SATAN EXTENDED ITS upper torso through the portal into the earthly realm. Its gaze scanned the area in front of the portal, taking in the killing field littered with carcasses of dead Demon Spawn. Then its eyes fixated on the six figures standing before it. The demon bent down and roared a guttural howl that sounded like the personification of a blast furnace.

Sook-kyoung glanced over at Jason. "What do we do now?"

Jason's voice wavered. "The rest of you grab the horses and get to a safe place."

"Why?"

"We failed. Once that thing crosses through, we don't stand a chance of closing the portal. At least you can save yourselves."

"What about you?" asked Haneef.

"I'm going to make one last attempt to shut it."

"So are we," Matthew replied.

"You're all crazy."

"Not necessarily." Haneef placed a hand on his friend's shoulder. "Maybe it's Allah's will that we'll succeed."

Standing erect, Satan proceeded through the portal. The remaining Golem moved to their right to allow the monstrosity to pass.

USTAGOV CIRCLED AROUND the corner of the portal at full gallop and charged across its front. The upper portion of Satan hovered above him. Adjusting his aim, the doctor threw the bag. It sailed over his head toward the shimmering surface of the—

With one swing of its massive right hand, Satan snatched the device in mid-air. As the horse passed, the demon used its left hand to rip Ustagov out of his saddle. The force of the blow knocked the wind out of him. The doctor hung limp in the creature's hand.

Sook-kyoung and Haneef responded the only way available to them. They raised their AK-47s and fired the remaining ammunition into the demon's face. Two rounds punctured its left eye. The demon roared again, this time in anger. Searching out the cause of its pain, it spotted the two humans with the weapons and flung the saddle bag at them.

Jason ran forward and jumped, catching it in mid-flight. He stumbled when he landed. Crouching into the fetal position, he hit the ground and rolled several times, protecting the anti-matter device. Jason stopped rolling a dozen feet from the two Golem, which were already moving toward him.

From off to the right, Father Belsario saw the perfect opportunity. The Golem were on the other side of the portal concentrating on Jason and Satan had been blinded in its left eye. He dashed toward the portal as the monstrosity raised its left leg to enter. Reaching up to his shoulder, the cleric went to slide off the saddle bag, only to find that the strap had become caught up in his cloak. He considered pausing to disentangle it, but by then it would be too late. Instead, he clutched the bag close to his chest and ran as fast as possible.

Closing his eyes and saying a silent prayer, Father Belsario jumped into the portal.

He experienced a moment of excruciating anguish as his body disintegrated upon contact with the surface, and then a blissful peace as his existence ended.

At the same time, the device's outer casing ruptured, releasing the frozen anti-matter inside. A blinding flash of light and a thunderous roar exploded from the portal, knocking Jason, Haneef, Sook-kyoung, and Matthew off their feet. Flames washed over the surface of the portal, enveloping Satan's torso.

The portal burned intensely for several seconds, consuming itself in the conflagration until it finally collapsed inward. When it did, it cut the monstrosity in half. Its upper body dropped onto the field with a heavy thud, sending up a cloud of dirt and dust. The shock wave spread out across the area, killing every demon except one.

"NO!" MEI YELLED as she watched the implosion of the gate. It was over. Everything she had struggled to achieve to bring salvation to a godless China, the sacrifices she had made in this endeavor, and the sacrifices she had forced others to make, were now all for naught. The travelers and the Unbelievers had won, and she knew well enough the fate that awaited the defeated.

Qiang ordered one of his horsemen to bind her hands at the wrist. Once completed, he tied the other end of the rope to his horse and headed out to round up the others.

THE SHOCKWAVE ROLLED across the landscape and washed past Sasha's group.

Jeanette gasped. It took her a moment to realize Lucifer pinned her to the ground, his jaws still around her neck. Her eyes scanned her surroundings until she spotted Sasha standing nearby, her saber ready to strike.

"Sorry," Jeanette said sheepishly.

Sasha stepped closer. "For what?"

"For trying to kill you."

"You remember that?"

Jeanette nodded as much as she could with a set of fangs so close to her arteries. "I was aware of what went on, but I couldn't stop myself."

Lilith made her way over, slowly and cautiously, and sniffed Jeanette. Her tail began wagging and she licked the young woman's face. Lucifer morphed back into his dog form and backed away, moving behind Sasha. Sasha sheathed her saber and held out her hand to Jeanette. Jeanette took it and Sasha helped her to her feet.

Ian stepped up to the two women. "I have a question."

"What is it?" Sasha asked.

"What are we going to do about her?"

To their surprise, Bai stood where she had been when the portal closed, alive yet greatly subdued. Vicky stood nearby with the machete, keeping a close watch on the demoness. Bai extended her hands by her side in supplication.

"I no longer pose a threat to you. I am at your mercy, so do with me what you please."

CHAPTER FORTY-THREE

JASON FELT A hand on his shoulder. At first, he feared it might be a Demon Spawn until he realized the hand gently shook him. He heard Sook-kyoung's voice. "Jason?"

"I'm fine." He moaned and opened his eyes. "The portals pack a punch when they close."

Sook-kyoung giggled, not at his bad joke but at him being alive.

Jason grew worried. "Where's Haneef?"

"He's okay." Sook-kyoung gestured behind her. "He's helping Ustagov."

As Jason got to his feet, he surveyed the area. Sure enough, the portal had collapsed. In front of it were the bodies of the four Golem killed in combat, the two that died when the portal closed, and Satan's half carcass, the severed end pouring blood into the soil. Haneef and Ustagov approached. The doctor limped, favoring his left leg, his arm wrapped around Haneef's shoulder for support.

"How badly are you hurt?" Jason asked when they got close.

"I'm in a lot of pain," said Ustagov. "Nothing is broken, and I don't think there's any internal damage. I should be fine in a few days. It's to be expected when you get ripped off your horse by a big-ass demon."

"You did an excellent job sneaking up on the portal while we distracted the Golem."

"Thanks." Ustagov removed his arm from around Haneef's shoulder and tried to stand. He winced under the pressure but did not collapse or ask for help. "I didn't do anything except get my butt kicked. Father Belsario closed the portal."

The cleric had sacrificed himself to deploy the anti-matter device. He knew Father Belsario and Gabriel would rejoin them soon; that did nothing to lessen the sense of loss.

Jason strung one of the two remaining backpacks containing an anti-matter device over his shoulder and handed the second to Sook-kyoung.

"Let's check on the others."

★　★　★

JASON FOUND THE rest of his team near the Sataners' camp. As he slid out of the saddle to greet them, Lucifer and Lilith rushed him, excited that their master had survived. The werehounds jumped on Jason, knocked him to the ground, and proceeded to lick each side of his face. They stopped only when Sasha came up and lovingly shoed them away so she could say hello. As she helped Jason to his feet, she pulled him close and held him tight for several seconds.

"I'm so glad you made it. When that thing came through the gate…." Sasha let her words trail off.

"I'm fine." Jason held her tight. Neither wanted to be the first to break their embrace.

Sasha let go first. "Where are Father Belsario and Gabriel?"

"Gabriel died battling the Golem," said Matthew. "Father Belsario closed the portal."

Sasha closed her eyes and prayed for them, especially the cleric. She knew all too well the agony he endured.

Jason approached the others. At first, Jeanette did not acknowledge him. Finally, she rushed into his arms and hugged him. She sobbed against his chest. Jason knew they were not tears of happiness. He held her tight, trying to comfort the young woman.

"Are you all right?"

Jeanette snorted. "I will be once we're out of here."

Jason patted her back and looked at the others. He was shocked to find Vicky with a makeshift bandage wrapped around her head, the left side stained with blood.

"What happened?"

"Bai attacked me. Ian cut up the trousers of one of the Sataners to use as a bandage."

Ustagov hobbled over and examined the dressing. "I'll patch that up when we get back to the factory."

"What factory?" Ian asked.

Ustagov dismissed the question with a shake of his head. "We'll fill you in on the way back."

Jason spotted the bloody remains of Antoine. He walked over, knelt on one knee, and closed his eyes. The deaths of every team member saddened Jason. Antoine's hit him harder than some of the others. The Moroccan had been a quiet man; tough as nails and fiercely loyal. Everyone on the expedition at one time or another owed their lives to him. Now he was gone. Antoine's absence would have a severe impact on their ability to continue their trek.

"You're at peace now, my old friend."

As Jason returned to the others, Sasha pointed to Bai. "What are we going to do with her?"

Jason reached out with his sixth sense to detect her aura. The malevolence he had felt when watching her at the decimation field had been stripped away. Her evil essence remained, only much more subdued since she had lost her powers. He also detected fear. Even more confusing than the change in her aura was his inability to determine Bai's essence. She did not reek of the tortured souls banished to the Under-world, nor did she read like the demons that originated in Hell. It was an entirely new category of being. Bai intrigued Jason, and he was determined to learn more about her.

Jason walked away. "We'll take her back to the factory with

us."

"Why?" Sasha asked.

"She's the only being from the other side we've encountered that is intelligent and can talk. I'm going to interrogate her and find out what's going on."

JASON CAUGHT UP with Qiang where the demons had savaged the Sataners. Of the cultists, only Mei and eleven children, all under the age of twelve, had survived. Qiang had ordered them taken back to the factory, Mei to be punished for her crimes and the children to be assimilated with and raised by the *Xiongnu*. When Mei saw Bai seated atop a horse, her arms bound and her legs lashed to the saddle, she averted her eyes and bowed her head in shame.

The *Xiongnu* suffered heavy casualties in the battle, though not nearly as bad as the Sataners. Out of the sixty-nine men who joined Jason in closing the portal, twenty-four survived. The *Xiongnu* scavenged what they could from the Sataners, taking their horses, tents, and supplies. They then arranged a funeral pyre in the middle of the battlefield for their fallen comrades, cremating their remains. The bodies of the Sataners were left to rot in the open, just like the Demon Spawn. Qiang said they deserved no better. Jason agreed.

The Demon Hunters dug graves for Antoine and Gabriel, choosing the hill overlooking the battlefield.

The funerary rituals were not completed until well after sunset. Normally, the group would have camped here for the night, but everyone wanted to get as far away from this area as possible. The *Xiongnu* and the Demon Hunters paid their last respects to their fallen friends before heading back to the factory. The children rode on horseback. Mei walked behind Qiang's horse, her hands bound in front of her and a rope around her neck and lashed to his saddle.

Jason departed last, spending a few extra minutes staring at the graves of Antoine and Gabriel. He sighed. It bothered him that Antoine's death had hit him so hard. Maybe the constant fighting had worn him down. After all, they had closed four portals in as many months, and they still had two more to go. The Demon Hunters had left a string of graves stretching across Europe and Russia and into northeast China, and he knew there would be many more left in their wake before they were through. Jason thought he had hardened himself against losing so many friends.

Or maybe it was the encounter with the Sataners that caused him to question their trek. For months, they had been battling their way across two continents, killing an array of Demon Spawn. Up until China, it had been a monster hunt. For the most part, the humans they had encountered had offered to help, like Reno and the Russians. This time, however, they had come up against humans who had decided to side with the demons. Jason had always thought the best of people, had assumed the few survivors that remained would band together to end the threat to mankind and rebuild society. His mind boggled at the idea that the Sataners would not only throw their lot in with the Demon Spawn but would sacrifice their fellow man in the process. How many others were out there struggling to keep the portals open? How many more groups such as Mei's would they encounter traveling to Japan and the States? How many were out there that he would never know about? It depressed him to think that if the Demon Hunters were successful in closing the portals, the world would be shared with people such as the Sataners.

Jason turned his horse around. He mentally said one last goodbye to Antoine and Gabriel and set off after the others. As he descended the hillock, one question continually ran through his mind.

Was this worth it?

Preview of *Shattered World IV*

JAPAN

Koto Nuclear Power Plant, off the coast of Tokyo in Tokyo Bay
Three days before the closure of the portal in China

THE FIVE-FOOT-TALL WEEDS swaying in the southwesterly wind obscured the view. It made Nori Mifune nervous. Or maybe it was the super typhoon approaching the east coast of Japan that threatened to strand them in this city of the damned until the weather system passed. More likely, a combination of the two. Mori had requested his team be allowed to abort the mission and return to Tokyo once conditions improved. Toshii had refused, stressing that they needed to get the most up-to-date readings, although he would not explain why. Nori demurred despite the feeling of impending doom that gnawed at him. The monthly trips to the power station were always dangerous. The overgrown weeds and grass had not been mowed since the apocalypse, offering the perfect hiding place. In calm weather, his team could move in close and obtain their readings, the presence of *jigoku no akuma,* or Hell Demons, given away by disturbances in the grass. Now that the entire field whipped about, those things could be racing in on them and no one would be aware of it until it was too late.

A hundred yards from the perimeter fence, Haruka raised the Model 4007A Geiger counter and switched it on. Its crackling thundered in the surrounding silence.

"What are the readings?" whispered Nori.

"It's .7 Sieverts per hour. Down from twelve Sieverts last month."

Nori stepped over to Akiko, who carried the JSDF Mobile Type II Multi-Purpose Broadband Radio. "Did you get that?"

"Yes."

"Radio the information back to Toshii."

"*Hai.*" Akiko slid the set off her shoulder, placed it on the ground, and dialed up their base.

Nori moved away from the others, his Howa Type 94 battle rifle in the high-ready position. Peering down the weapon's scope, he swept the weapon in a slow one-hundred-and-eighty-degree arc, watching for disturbances in the wavering grass that might indicate an approaching Hell Demon. Isoruku joined him, his back to Nori as he scanned the area to their rear. Nori expected one of the creatures to rush them at any moment. He inhaled deep, held his breath for ten seconds, and slowly exhaled, hoping to ease the tension. It did little good.

Every few seconds, Nori glanced over at Akiko. She spoke quietly but animatedly to someone on the other end of the line. He mentally ordered her to hurry up. After close to a minute, she waved him over. "Toshii wants to talk to you."

Nori took the microphone. "Yes?"

"I need readings from inside the plant."

"The last time we tried, the radiation levels were lethal, and we had to abort."

"I know," Toshii admitted. "At that time the levels outside were much higher. I need to know if they've also decreased inside."

Nori said nothing, knowing full well the implications of entering the plant.

"Are you still there?"

"Yes," Nori sighed. "We'll get them."

"Thank you. Good luck, *Nori-san.*"

Nori handed the microphone to Akiko. As she packed up the radio and slid it back over her shoulder, Nori stared across the field. Two hundred feet away stood the perimeter chain link fence and another two hundred feet beyond that the Koto Nuclear Power Plant. The four cooling towers marked the location of the reactors—two under construction and two finished, one of those having collapsed during the formation of the portal. The structures were cold and sterile, appearing even more ominous in the dull light of the cloudy afternoon. The interior of the facility would be even less hospitable. And deadly.

After briefing the others on what Toshii expected, Nori led his team toward the chain link fence. Each held their weapon in the high-ready position, on the lookout for any potential danger. When ten feet from the perimeter fence, Nori used the overgrown grass as cover as he led his team to a collapsed segment of fence they used to gain access to the plant. He paused. The concrete approaches to the facility allowed a clear view of the compound. Several thousand of the damned staggered mindlessly around the grounds. With their dried, leathery skin and various stages of disrobement, they reminded Nori of zombies from horror movies, only these nightmares were real. Most of the damned lingered near the front of the facility and jammed the causeway to the mainland. Several strays sauntered around the rear of the compound, too few to pose any danger, and no other Hell Demons were visible. Nori hoped they would find the same inside the plant. He snapped his fingers to get the other's attention and signaled for them to proceed. They dashed across the approaches. A few of the damned spotted them and stumbled in their direction, too far away to be of any concern. Reaching Reactor Building Four, Nori led the way along the exterior wall toward the rear façade and to the emergency exit they had left unlocked on a previous visit. Isoruku switched on his head-mounted flashlight, pulled open the metal door, and rushed inside. A tense few seconds passed before he yelled, "Clear!"

The others rushed in, each switching on their own flashlight before entering. Reactor Four had been in the earliest stages of development, so they stood in an enclosed construction site that encompassed the foundation of the future plant. The beams from their flashlights barely illuminated beyond one hundred feet, leaving the area beyond a total mystery. Nori half expected Hell Demons to charge from the shadows. He tapped down that image before it overwhelmed him. The crackling of the Geiger counter brought him back to their more immediate fear.

"The readings here are higher than outside," said Haruka.

"How much?"

"Still less than one Sievert per hour. We'll need readings near the portal."

"Is that necessary?" Isoruku asked.

"It is." Nori cursed under his breath. "Follow me."

Nori crossed the construction site to a tunnel twenty feet square and proceeded down it. Haruka kept the Geiger counter on to take readings as they moved. Nori concentrated on its crackling, hoping it would distract him from thinking about what might be lurking in the shadows, especially the *dāku-kurōrā*, the dark crawlers that roamed the plant's interior. Two other teams had encountered them; one had never been heard from again and the other had one survivor who made it out and radioed back, rambling insanely about what he had witnessed before the damned overran him.

As they proceeded deeper into the complex, the counter registered only slight increases. It took several minutes to reach a steel radiation door twenty feet square, beyond which sat the quadrangle at the center of the facility where the access tunnels to the four reactors converged.

Isoruku stepped up and pressed the green OPEN button. Nothing happened. "We're not going any further."

"Yes, we are." Nori shined his flashlight around until the beam fell open a wall-mounted steel box near the door. He unlatched and lowered the lid, revealing two hand cranks.

Swinging his battle rifle over his shoulder, Nori removed them and handed one to Isoruku. He inserted the geared end into a slotted opening on the right side of the door and motioned for Isoruku to do the same on the left. The two men turned the cranks counterclockwise. At first, the door did not budge. Both men leaned into the cranks, pushing their weight against them. After a few seconds, the door groaned and rose ten inches. Akiko stepped back and aimed her Howa at the widening gap, ready to shoot anything that came through. When the door reached the halfway point, she bowed and scanned her light into the quadrangle. Once certain nothing lurked inside, she waved on the others.

On the opposite wall of the quadrangle was the radiation door to the tunnel complex beneath completed Reactor Building Three, the second completed reactor as well as the one that had partially collapsed. Off to the left, two more tunnels led to Reactor Buildings One and Two, which were still under construction; the door to Reactor Building Two was rolled up, exposing the tunnel.

Still holding the hand crank, Nori stepped up to the radiation door for Reactor Building Three and inserted the geared end into the slotted opening on the right. Isoruku did the same on the left. With a nod from Nori, the two raised the door two feet.

The crackling on Haruka's Geiger counter spiked.

Nori stopped. "How dangerous is it?"

"Hang on." Haruka squinted to read the lighted display. "I'm trying to get an accurate reading."

Nori detected another sound accompanying the crackling, a noise faint yet distinct. He tapped Haruka on the shoulder. "Shut that off."

"I don't have the—"

"Do it!"

The crackling died out, only to be replaced by a clicking, like claws scraping against metal. It multiplied and grew louder.

"Lower the door." Isoruku turned the crank in the opposite direction.

"There's no time. Fall ba—"

Haruka screamed. Nori spun his head-mounted flashlight around in time to see the woman being dragged under the door, frantically scratching at the floor, leaving behind three torn-off fingernails and accompanying trails of blood. A moment later, Haruka screamed in such agony that Nori's blood turned cold. Dropping to one knee, he aimed his Howa through the gap and fired off the entire twenty-five-round magazine. High-pitched shrieks emanated from the other side and the clicking intensified.

Akiko had retreated down Reactor Four's access tunnel, pausing at the threshold. She raised her Howa and aimed at the gap. "Come on!"

Isoruku dropped prone in the quadrangle, firing three-round bursts at the dark crawlers. Before Nori could order his friend to fall back, Isoruku cried out as a line formed on his left arm below the shoulder and cut its way through flesh, tissue, and bone. He grabbed the stump with his good hand. Crying from pain and fear, he struggled to his feet. Something emerged from the shadows under the door and grabbed Isoruku by the leg. In a movement so rapid it appeared as a blur, the creature dragged Isoruku through the gap. His screams echoed down the access tunnel until they could no longer be heard over the din of the clicking.

"We have to move now!" yelled Akiko.

Nori saw a shadow rush out from under the door, climb the wall, and race across the ceiling above Akiko. It dropped on her, extinguishing the head-mounted flashlight. A grotesque slurping emanated from the creature, followed by cracking as it applied pressure to Akiko's skull. In the limited glare from his own flashlight, Nori watched as she howled and thrashed about, rushing down the tunnel and slamming her head against the wall to dislodge the dark crawler. When that did not work,

Akiko raised her Howa and fired on the creature, killing herself in the process.

Something brushed by Nori's leg, slashing through his pants and tearing a four-inch gash in his left calf. He did not see what caused the wound. Limping across the quadrangle, he crouched to get under the partially-opened door and hobbled down the access tunnel. Behind him, the clicking grew louder. Nori made the mistake of glancing over his shoulder to see how close the creatures were, and in doing so tripped over Akiko's body. He hit the floor with a thud, knocking the wind out of him. The Howa flew out of his hands, clattering down the tunnel into the dark. His flashlight slipped off his head, spinning across the floor until it came to rest against the wall, its beam aimed into the quadrangle. A swarm of dark crawlers rushed toward him.

Nori's last thought was, *this is what Hell must be like.*

A Thank You to My Readers

I've been working on the *Shattered World* saga for five years. This project has been a labor of love; I'm very pleased with where the story has taken me so far and am excited about where it's going. Hopefully you've also enjoyed the journey. I consider myself a storyteller and, like any good bard, want to keep my readers entertained so they'll come back for more. That's why every novel in the series has more demons, more unique characters, and more action than the previous ones. My goal is to keep you up way past your bedtime because you cannot put down the book. It's my way of saying thank you for standing by me all these years.

If you liked *Shattered World III: China*, please tell your friends about the book, give me a shout out on your social media, and/or and review it on Amazon and Goodreads. The review does not have to be long—just a rating and a sentence or two about why you enjoyed it. The more reviews *Shattered World III: China* receives, the more opportunity others have of discovering the book. If you haven't read yet *Shattered World I: Paris* or *Shattered World II: Russia*, the first two novels in the series, they're available on Amazon, Kindle, and Kindle Unlimited.

The *Shattered World* saga will continue. The next novel takes place in Japan and has one of the most evil and bone-chilling demons I've conceived of yet—dark crawlers. And, as always, if you like a particular character(s), the chances are he/she won't survive.

Acknowledgments

I want to thank Michele Thompson for her excellent editorial skills and for catching the things I missed in the final draft; this is the third book she has edited for me and she has helped make each one a success. Uwe Jarling and Julie Nicholls created the cover art and, as with the first and second books, their work is phenomenal. Uwe takes my visions of the characters and demons and brings them to life. Many thanks also to Petar Dekic for providing the maps so my readers can follow the adventures of the Demon Hunters.

I would be remiss if I didn't thank my Beta readers, the unsung heroes of writers. After you review and revise the original draft half a dozen times, you become blind to some of the errors in it. Lloyd Kerns and Brian Marek-Murray read the manuscript and pointed out grammatical/spelling errors, plot inconsistencies, and things that did not work. Their efforts to carefully pick through the story made the novel much better. I also owe a huge debt of gratitude to Lisa Holland Mastandrea who reviewed the final draft before publication and caught those damnable spelling/grammar errors that always remain so well hidden during the editing and revision stages.

Although he did not play an active role in helping me write *Shattered World III: China*, I need to thank my dear friend (who sadly is no longer with us) and colleague, Paul Simon. Paul and I met when we were stationed in Seoul, South Korea in the early 1990s and, as kindred spirits, became best friends. I visited him in 1999 while he was stationed at the Shenyang Consulate. We spent a week touring Manchukuo, the territory that once belonged to the puppet government of Pu Yi, who collaborated with the Imperial Japanese occupation forces in World War II, which today is Manchuria. We toured Shenyang, Harbin, Changchun, Unit 731, and drove or took trains all over the countryside. It was one of the most fascinating trips I've ever taken, and I became very familiar with the people and the region. When I decided to locate the portal in China, there was no question I would pick Manchuria. Thanks, Paul.

Finally, the biggest thanks go to my family, human and furry. My wife Alison, who is also a writer, understands and shares my passion, and never complains when I abandon her to write (I think it's partly because she gets to control the TV remote). My Boxers Walther and Bella are the inspirations for Lucifer and Lilith, although neither of them fight Demon Spawn (although Bella has lost four battles with a porcupine and a skunk). My cats Archer and Michonne stay with me in my basement study and allow me to work after I'm done playing with, petting, and giving them treats (note to other writers: don't get a touch-screen computer when you have a cat with a swishing tail who shares your desk). Although they all want to be with me, my family gives me the time I need to write and never holds my self-imposed isolation against me. I couldn't do this without their love and support.

Author's Bio

Scott M. Baker was born and raised in Everett, Massachusetts and spent twenty-three years in northern Virginia working for the Central Intelligence Agency. Scott is now retired and lives outside of Concord, New Hampshire along with his wife and stepdaughter. He has written *Nurse Alissa vs the Zombies and Nurse Alissa vs. the Zombies II: Escape*, the first in a multi-book series focusing on a young woman learning how to survive in a world overrun by the living dead; *Shattered World I: Paris* and *Shattered World II: Russia*, the first two books in his five-book young adult fantasy series; *The Vampire Hunters* trilogy, about humans fighting the undead in Washington D.C.; *Rotter World, Rotter Nation*, and *Rotter Apocalypse*, his post-apocalyptic zombie saga; *Yeitso*, his homage to the giant monster movies of the 1950s that he loved watching as a kid; as well as a several zombie-themed novellas and anthologies.

Please check out Scott's social media accounts for the latest information on future books, upcoming events, and other fun stuff.

Blog: scottmbakerauthor.blogspot.com
Facebook: facebook.com/groups/397749347486177
Twitter: @vampire_hunters
Instagram: scottmbakerwriter

www.ingramcontent.com/pod-product-compliance
Lightning Source LLC
Chambersburg PA
CBHW071304250626
47159CB00004B/1303